WHEN YOUR SOUL MATE IS THE MAN YOU LOATHED AT FIRST SIGHT…

Veronica Diaz loves her career, her friends and the great outdoors – she has no room in her life for men. In fact, she knows there are only two types of men in the world: players and wanna-be players and she wants nothing to do with any of them.

So when a psychic informs Veronica that her fated soul mate is Frederick Knight "The King of Players," Veronica does what any sensible woman would do – she runs.

A twist of fate lands Veronica in the depths of a pitch-black cave system with a man she's never met and can't see. As Veronica and Sam struggle to survive they open up, share their secrets, and risk their lives for each other. Soon Veronica starts to wonder if maybe not all men are players, and maybe she can trust Sam enough to fall in love.

The only problem: Sam is actually Frederick Knight. The man Veronica swore she'd never, ever, ever love. In fact, she loathed him at first sight.

And if they make it out of the cave alive, and Veronica sees him for the first time, she'll loathe him again. Won't she?

But maybe, sometimes you can only see who someone really is when you can't see them at all? And maybe you can only fall in love when it's *not* at first sight?

ALSO BY SARAH READY

Stand Alone Romances:

The Fall in Love Checklist

Hero Ever After

Soul Mates in Romeo Romance Series:

Chasing Romeo

Love Not at First Sight

Find more books by Sarah Ready at:

www.sarahready.com/romance-books

Sign up to receive bonus content, exclusive epilogues and more at:
www.sarahready.com/newsletter

love not at first sight

SARAH READY

CROWN

W.W. CROWN BOOKS
An imprint of Swift & Lewis Publishing LLC
www.wwcrown.com

This book is a work of fiction. All the characters and situations in this book are fictitious. Any resemblance to situations or persons living or dead is purely coincidental. Any reference to historical events, real people, or real locations are used fictitiously.

Library of Congress Control Number: 2021910085
ISBN: 978-1-954007-11-6 (eBook)
ISBN: 978-1-954007-12-3 (pbk)
ISBN: 978-1-954007-14-7 (hbk)
ISBN: 978-1-954007-13-0 (large print)

love not at first sight

1

VERONICA

I'VE ALWAYS KNOWN two things—that life is an adventure and that love makes you weak. If you want to keep having fun in life then you need to stay as far away from love as possible.

"Veronica, come down from there," Miss Erma calls. She's in her eighties and she's been ordering the good people of Romeo around for so many decades that her voice is full of command.

Too bad.

I ignore her and keep climbing. I'm fifty feet up, wedged against a sheer rockface. I reach into the chalk pouch clipped to my shorts and dust more chalk on my hands, then I reach for the next handhold.

"Veronica," she calls in a long, high voice. She even waves a hand at me.

Nope. Not going to answer.

Don't get me wrong. I respect Erma and think of her as family. She's my best friend's great-aunt and has been a staple in my life since I was a baby. Her oatmeal cookies are to die for and she's loads of fun. But I live in terror of her. Absolute terror.

Why would I be scared of an eighty-year-old five-foot-nothing woman in a kimono? Because. She's a bona fide soul mate seer. Last year she predicted the identity of my best friend's soul mate and it turned Chloe's life upside down. Okay, in a good way, since Chloe's a diehard romantic, but still. I'm not.

Speaking of... "Chloe, you are in the best friend doghouse," I yell. She stands on the rocky trail, fifty feet below me.

"Hey. I didn't tell her you were here," Chloe protests. She puts more slack on the belay rope. She's my climbing buddy. She manages the belay so that if I fall, the device catches and I don't fall far. Because, as much as I love adventure and adrenaline, I don't love plunging to my death.

I glance down and try to see Chloe's face. She's never been able to lie to me, but I can't see her from so far up. She's hidden by the shadow of the craggy rock and the low brush around her.

Doesn't matter. I'll climb to the top and hike out without ever having to see Miss Erma. I lift my leg and edge my foot into a foothold. I'm in climbing shoes and my foot fits perfectly in the small crack. I boost myself and grab another handhold. The top is only ten more feet and a couple tricky maneuvers away. I can do this. I wipe away the sweat on my forehead and dust my hands with more chalk.

"Veronica," calls Erma.

"Nope. No thank you," I shout down. "Not interested."

I hear Miss Erma cluck and watch her shake her head.

I can't believe she actually came all the way out to the gorge to harass me about my soul mate. I mean, I have been avoiding her calls and her hints and her knocking at my door for about two weeks now, but still...

Enough is enough.

"Miss Erma," I call down. "I don't want to fall in love. I don't want a soul mate."

"But why not, dear? I've seen him, he's—"

"No thank you," I interrupt. I wish my hands were free so I could hold them over my ears.

"But why not?" she calls.

"Because love makes you weak." I say it quietly but somehow she hears me.

"No, dear. Love makes you strong."

I disagree. I have a whole lifetime of experience that says otherwise.

Love makes you weak is my motto.

I keep climbing. I slowly make my way to the top. Every now and then I look down. Erma chats with an animated and happy Chloe. Darn, it looks like Erma isn't planning on leaving until she tells me her "news." I make it to the top of the cliff, plant my hands on the rock and boost myself over.

Relief spreads through me and I let out a long sigh.

I'm safe for at least a little longer.

Chloe and Erma are still deep in conversation. Neither notices that I made it to the top. So, I do something that I am in no way ashamed of. Not one bit.

I unclip the climbing rope, step out of my harness, drop it to the ground...and run.

I run two miles all the way back to my apartment in downtown Romeo.

Chloe, being the awesome best friend that she is, will grab my equipment and make sure it gets home.

❦

"What about that one?" asks Ferran. She points to a thirty-something man in a pink checkered shirt and gray slacks.

Me, Chloe, Jessie and Ferran are at our bi-weekly girls' night out at Juliet's Wine Bar. We're playing the 'can you pick out the player' game.

"Player," I say. "Too easy."

Jessie and Ferran laugh, but they believe me. It's rare that I'm ever wrong about a man.

"How do you know?" Chloe asks. She frowns, she's such a trusting romantic that she always fell for the players and the sleaze balls and the jerks. Luckily, she found her soul mate and he's actually a decent guy. Thank goodness.

I tense up, because thinking about Chloe's soul mate reminds me that Erma's after me like a bloodhound on the trail.

"But how do you know?" asks Chloe again. She always gives people the benefit of the doubt. Me...I never do.

"Because," I say. I wave my hand at the guy. "I can see his wedding ring tan line from here. Too obvious. Ferran, I know you like men in pink, but he's married."

"Ugh. Darn my pink shirt kryptonite."

We laugh and I look around the wine bar and take in the scene. It's unusually crowded. The barstools at the tasting bar are full, and all of the leather booths are packed tight. There are even couples and small groups standing around the wine barrel tables. Juliet's serves mostly local New York wines, and some Californian, there's a few French wines available, but Juliet prefers to support local wineries. I take another sip of my Riesling.

"Is there any guy here that's decent?" asks Ferran. "It's been months since I broke up with Craig and I'm really in the mood for a one-nighter."

I raise my eyebrows. Ferran is more workaholic than romance-aholic, a one-night stand isn't really her style.

She scowls. "What? I have needs."

I shrug. You can't argue with the truth. But…"Let me remind you of my philosophy on men."

Ferran groans and runs her hands through her curly black hair. "Not again."

"Oh boy," says Jessie.

She's been hearing this recital for years, they all have, but it never hurts to have a refresher.

"There are only two types of men in the world," I say.

I hold up a finger. "Players." I hold up another finger. "And wanna-be players." I point around the bar. "Player," I say, pointing to a man in baggy jeans and a hoody. "Wanna-be player," I say, pointing at his friend who is enviously watching him hit on a woman in a short dress.

I go around the bar, pointing out each man. "Player. Wanna-be player. Player. Player. Wanna-be. And…player."

"So, no one," says Ferran.

Chloe rolls her eyes. "Don't believe her. She's scarred from her childhood. There are plenty of nice guys out there."

"Name one," I say.

Chloe huffs and looks offended. "My husband."

"Oh, right. Well yeah. But, he's not…hmmm," I backpedal, "maybe there are three types of men in the world. Players, wanna-be players, and your husband."

Chloe snorts and I know I'm forgiven.

Chloe sets a hand on her rounded stomach and gets that happy, starry-eyed expression she's had for months now. That's right, my best friend is drinking juice at a wine bar, because she's gonna be a mom. And me, I'm going to be a godmother. The baby's due in two months. I can't wait to meet her. But sometimes, when Chloe has me put my hand on her stomach to feel the baby kick, I have to admit, I don't feel joy like I should, I feel…lonely.

Alone and lonely.

I point across the room at a dark haired man in a business suit, "there. He's fine."

"Oh. No. No way. Uh uh," Jessie says. Her brow draws down and she glares at the man leaning against the bar. Jessie is the town librarian and she usually likes everyone, so her vehement dislike of the guy is weird.

"You know him?" I ask.

"Unfortunately. That's Will Williams. Your man radar failed on him Veronica, he's the opposite of fine." Jessie glares at the man's back and I get the impression that she really doesn't like him, and also, that she's not about to talk about him.

There's a pause as we all look at the guy then turn away.

"Anyway," Ferran says, "let's stop beating around the bush and talk about Erma."

I swallow the last of my wine and pour another glass from the bottle. "Let's not," I say.

Chloe grins. "Come on, Vee. Give in gracefully. Aunt Erma's seen your soul mate, there's nothing you can do."

I look at my friends. Chloe, of course, is excited for me, although she's trying to hide it because she knows I don't want a soul mate. Ferran has a half-smile because she usually finds the humor in awful situations. Jessie looks worried for me because she's sweet like that. I take another fortifying swallow of the wine.

"I don't want to know," I say. No matter how alone I feel, I don't want to find the man I'm supposed to love only to be hurt by him. It's not worth it.

"But why?" asks Chloe. "You don't have to marry him. Or even love him. But wouldn't you like to know, just *know* who your soul mate is?"

"No," I say. I don't even need to think about it.

Ever since I learned that Erma was a bona fide soul mate psychic I've been scared that she'd see mine. She's foretold, who knows, probably hundreds of soul mates, and they all, every single one, has gotten married, had little babies, and lived happily ever after. Erma is a force of nature. Chloe has a family heirloom, this thick book full of photographs of all the happy couples Erma has matched. Chloe was Erma's latest soul mate vision. And now...apparently I am.

I don't want it though. I think I'll be the one person, the one vision of Erma's that fails.

"But why?" asks Jessie. "If Erma told me my soul mate I'd be ecstatic. I'd do everything in my power to win him."

"Not me," says Ferran. "I have a career. Goals. I don't need a man to ruin my life."

"Exactly," I say. "Love makes you weak."

Chloe shakes her head. "Love makes you strong."

I raise an eyebrow at Chloe. She's the only one at this table who knows the reasons why I don't trust men and why I think that love is the worst thing that can happen to a woman.

When I was little, cute with blonde hair in pigtails, and frilly dresses, my dad used to take me around and pretend to be a single dad so he could land sympathetic women. He called me his lucky charm. Every weekend, from age three to nine, my dad schlepped me around playgrounds, parks, grocery stores, diners, and libraries, using his single dad schtick to great effect. He hooked up with countless women lured in by the hapless single dad routine.

Here's the kicker. He wasn't single. He and my mom were still married.

But my mom knew what he was doing and she didn't stop him. She said she *loved* him too much. She couldn't leave him. It hurt too much to go and she couldn't stop him. So she stayed. My mom, who had once been vibrant and strong, became weak.

After I hit age nine, had a growth spurt and got braces, my

dad couldn't use the cute little girl and single dad scheme anymore. So, he came up with a different schtick, I don't know what. But I'd seen enough, all player routines are the same. I recognize them to this day.

There's the "I'm so misunderstood" routine.

The "you aren't like other women" routine.

And the "I feel so different with you" lie.

The "only you understand me," or "my ex was psycho," (except how are *all* the exes psycho?), or "we're just friends," (trust me, they aren't just friends), or "I love you," which is the biggest play of all and is almost always whispered right before he lifts up your skirt and goes for it. Men trade love for sex, women trade sex for love. It's not an even trade.

Never trust a man. The minute you do, you make yourself weak.

Ask my mom.

After my dad died we found his little black book. In it there were nine hundred seventy-seven names of the women he had "dated."

My mom and I had an argument after finding that book. I told her she was weak for never leaving my dad, and she said I didn't understand. I didn't. I haven't spoken to her since.

I set down my wine glass and force out a smile. "It doesn't matter. I'm not going to get married. Ever."

No matter how lonely I feel, or how much my heart squeezes when I feel Chloe's baby girl kicking. It doesn't matter.

"What will you do when Erma catches up to you?" asks Jessie.

"Run."

Jessie and Ferran laugh and Chloe rolls her eyes.

"You say that now," Chloe says. "But you'll see. This is a good thing."

"Agree to disagree," I say.

"When you find *the one*, Vee, it's the best feeling in the whole world."

Ferran shakes her head. "What if Erma says her soul mate is some creep? Or a toad? What if he's—"

"A player," I say.

The words are like acid in my gut. That's my worst nightmare. To be in love with a player and not to be able to walk away. To remain in a relationship with a cheating, narcissistic player because of *love*. If I could guarantee that he wouldn't be a player...but I can't.

"He won't be," says Chloe.

"You have absolute faith in fate," I say.

"Of course I do."

"I don't," I say. "Fate has a sick sense of humor and Erma is her maniacal handmaiden..."

I trail off. Jessie shakes her head and Chloe's eyes go wide.

"She's behind me, isn't she?" I ask.

"Uh huh," says Ferran.

"Hi Miss Erma," says Jessie.

Slowly, I turn my head and look up at Erma. This is it. Two weeks of running and she's finally caught me.

"Veronica," says Erma in a scolding voice. "I never imagined you a coward. Running away like that." She shakes her finger at me.

My cheeks heat. I'm going to claim it's the wine making them flush, not embarrassment.

"I don't want to know," I say. "That's not cowardly. I just don't want to know."

She throws her hands up in the air and her bracelets clack on her wrists. "That's what I've been trying to tell you," she says. "You can't run away from this. He's coming."

"What?" I ask. The hair on the back of my neck stands on end. I don't want this.

"He's coming to Romeo and you won't be able to run away."

"Umm, Aunt Erma? Who's coming?" asks Chloe.

"Her soul mate, dear."

"When?" I ask. Forewarned is forearmed. I can avoid him. I can...

"Tomorrow," says Erma.

"How do you know?" Ferran asks.

Erma drops the *Romeo Record*, the town's weekly paper on the table. "Because it says so right here."

On the front page is a picture of the old Reddington Mansion. I scan the article. It's been sold to a new owner.

"Who bought it?" asks Jessie.

Erma pins me with her shrewd gaze and if I could get up and run, I would. But I feel stuck to the chair.

"Frederick Knight," she says.

My stomach bottoms out.

"Oh no," Chloe says in a horrified whisper.

"But..." Jessie says.

"Jeez," Ferran says.

I stare at Erma, shaking my head in denial.

"Aunt Erma, maybe you're...wrong?" asks Chloe in a hopeful voice.

Aunt Erma purses her lips. She's never wrong. Never, ever, ever wrong. She's been predicting soul mates for decades and she's never made a mistake. I stare at Erma and my friends in a daze. The room tilts and my mind must be fuzzy from the wine because I thought she'd said...

"Did you say Frederick Knight?" I ask.

Erma smiles and nods. "That's right, dear."

I grab the edge of the table to steady myself.

"Jeez," Ferran says again.

But then, a surge of clarity busts through my mind. Chloe had this misunderstanding too. It could be any Frederick

Knight, any Frederick Knight in the whole world, not necessarily…

Erma lifts her hand and points at the flat screen TV hanging over the bar.

"That man," she says.

Oh. Oh no.

There's no misunderstanding.

Acid burns through my chest and down to my stomach.

Fate, with her cruel sense of humor, has matched me with Frederick Knight, the most unrepentant, detestable, horrible poster child for players that ever existed.

"Never," I say. "I will never, ever fall in love with *that* man. The *King of Players*. I loathe him. I've never met him and I *loathe* him. He's reprehensible."

The King of Players. That's the press's nickname for billionaire bad boy Frederick Knight. He's the idol that all players bow down to and worship.

I watch the TV screen with growing horror. He's in a hot tub, wearing a panama hat and aviator sunglasses. He's holding a champagne flute and a bottle of champagne. There are six topless models in the hot tub with him. He laughs as they pour bottles of bubbly over his bronzed skin. One of the models starts to lick his chin as he grins and motions the others over. The clip cuts away.

I make a desperate sound, like an animal in a trap.

"Oh no," says Chloe. "This isn't good."

"Jeez," Ferran says.

"Your soul mate is Frederick Knight? The billionaire?" Jessie asks. I can hear the worry in her voice.

"It doesn't matter," I choke out. My voice is thick with tears.

"Why not?" asks Chloe.

"Because," I say. "I will never speak to him. Never meet him.

Never have anything to do with that...that...*player*. I will never love that man."

"You can't fight it," Chloe says sadly. "Trust me."

Quickly, I push back from the table and stand. "Maybe I can't fight it," I say. "But I can run." I take a step back. Erma narrows her eyes on me, but I'm past caring if she thinks I'm a coward or not.

"I'm taking two weeks off work," I tell Chloe. We're partners in an incredibly successful independent greeting card company. She's the artistic talent and I'm the business brains. "I'm due for a vacation and you can man the ship."

"Allllright," Chloe says uncertainly.

"I'm going...on a hike. I'm going backcountry camping on the White Pine Trail. I'll...I'll... Text me when he leaves, okay?"

Because a player like Frederick Knight won't stay long in small-town Romeo. He couldn't possibly. He'll get bored, miss his hot tubs and models, and run back to whatever obscene circus he lives in.

I don't wait for my friends to confirm. I hightail it out of the bar. A little unsteady, a lot scared. My worst nightmare, this is my worst nightmare coming to life.

I'm going to go pack my backpack and get myself so lost in the backwoods that fate will never be able to find me. Guaranteed.

2

———

SAM

THERE'S an uncomfortable truth that I have to face, I have the whole world at my fingertips and...it means nothing. The terrace of my penthouse overlooking Central Park teems with Clara's friends. Models she's done shows with, reality TV stars, producers, sycophants.

"What are you thinking?" asks Clara. She comes up next to me and sets her wine glass on the stone ledge. I'm in sunglasses and a ball cap, pants and a shirt, overdressed for her spur-of-the-moment party. The rest of the men here are in bathing suits.

Clara's in a tiny gold bikini with a see-through string holding the sides and back up. She leans forward and brushes her fingers through my hair. Even though she's one of the top working runway models and recently lauded as one of the most beautiful people in the world, her touch does nothing for me.

"I think it's time for you to go home," I say.

"Oh please," she says. She drags her finger down my chest. "You're always in the mood for a party. Just last week you threw that impromptu trip to Aspen for me and my friends, and—"

"Not today."

I know how I look and I know how she and the rest of the world perceive me. After twenty years of being a scrawny, pasty, computer-loving nerd I filled out, grew up and in the words of my ex-wife "got hot." I'm the ugly duckling personified, except I loathe being the swan.

Clara gives me a heavy-lidded look and smiles.

I shake my head. "Go home, Clara."

"What's wrong with you?"

I look at her friends. They've raided my wine collection and ordered from dozens of restaurants. The porter keeps bringing up bags of food. Some of the women have stripped to dip in the pool or lounge in the hot tub. The sound system blasts an obnoxious techno beat, something you'd hear at fashion week or a euro-style club.

I rub my forehead.

"It's not a good day."

"What? Only make a few million today? Did your stock not do as well as you wanted?"

"Clara, I think it's time to say goodbye."

She draws in a sharp breath, then she pretends to misunderstand. "We only just got here."

I shake my head.

"But why?" She tilts her head, then drags her finger down my arm. "You're rich. I'm beautiful. We're perfect together."

She's right. This is how it's always been done. If a man is wealthy then his prize is a beautiful woman. If a woman is beautiful her prize is a wealthy man. It works best when both people realize that the only reason they're together is because of this age-old agreement.

"You don't even like me," I tell her.

She raises her eyebrows in an expression of surprise. "I do."

"Name one thing you like about me."

"Your Learjet."

I fight back a snort. "What else?"

"Your house in the Hamptons."

I shake my head. "No. Those aren't me. What do you like about me?"

She gives me a condescending look. "You're being ridiculous. I like you. I like the things you have, what we do." She waves her hand at the party.

"Like this?" I gesture around the terrace. Most of her friends are skinny dipping in the pool. Someone has ordered a ten-gallon bucket of mint chip ice cream and a few people are body painting each other with it.

"Exactly like this."

I take in the scene. She's right. For the past five years I've lived a life of public dissipation. I've become exactly who I set out to be. A jerk. A terrible person.

"If I told you…" I say in a serious voice.

"Yes?" asks Clara, leaning closer.

"…that I actually prefer quiet nights at home. That I like to read science fiction and do sudoku puzzles. That I spend hours taking apart old computers or clocks or cameras and putting them back together. What if I told you that I'm an introvert and I don't like parties or going clubbing and I don't like champagne baths or ten-thousand-dollar dinners or…if I told you that I'm actually a…geek. What would you say?"

Clara watches me with a look of confusion that turns to shock, then finally she starts to laugh. "Oh my gosh. You had me going. So earnest. Did you practice that speech? You are so ridiculous. Jeez. *I'm a geek.* Yeah right. That's like saying the Statue of Liberty is a piece of junk. You're gorgeous, sexy, wealthy…you don't care about anything, you just want to have a good time. That's why I like you. We're two peas in a pod. We could have this kind of fun for the rest of our lives."

That's what I'm afraid of.

I look at the party, at the waste and the materialism of my life, at the mess of it all. I slip my hand in my pocket and feel the torn edges of the newspaper clipping. It practically burns against my fingers. I don't have to read it, I know what it says.

BioTech CEO Garrett Parker and his wife Louisa Parker announce the birth of their daughter, Ella Louisa Parker, at Lenox Hill Hospital, New York, NY.

I yank my hand from the clipping. I close my eyes and try to block out the ache. Louisa, my ex-wife, and Garrett, my ex-business partner and ex-best-friend, had a daughter.

Hell.

They...she...I thought I'd burned away the grief, the hurt, but one little announcement, the birth of an innocent child, has brought back everything.

If gallons of champagne and wine, parties in Aspen and the Hamptons, trips to Monaco, scores of girlfriends, and a life of waste couldn't erase this feeling...nothing can.

"I'll go," I say to Clara. "I'm going out."

"No, don't. We'll have fun. I can send them away. We can enact your fantasy, beauty and the geek."

"Clara..." I pause. This needs to be said, and the sooner the better. I can't drag this out anymore. "We're done, Clara. Our relationship is over." For the first time since my divorce, I feel guilt. I dragged this on too long. I typically keep my dating relationships to less than a week, Clara has been with me for nearly three weeks. Too long.

"I refuse to accept that," she says. Her mouth sets in a hard line and her chin juts out.

"We're done," I say.

Her eyes narrow and she realizes that I'm serious. That we're through.

"Fine. You're right," she says and she shrugs. "I don't like you. You're cold, arrogant, closed-off...a grade-A prick. You look like every woman's fantasy lover and you have more money than Midas, but none of that matters because...because it comes with *you*. And *you* are fundamentally unlikeable."

I nod. The newspaper clipping burns hot in my pocket. What Clara's saying...I've heard it before. Whether I've been a computer-loving awkward teen, a dorky twenty-something, or a billionaire sex symbol, the part that's *me*...that bit is never wanted.

"I'm going out," I say. "You and your friends will be gone by the time I get back."

I walk away. Clara picks up her wine glass and throws her Bordeaux at my back. The lukewarm wine runs through my hair and soaks the back of my shirt.

"WHAT HAPPENED TO YOU?" MY SISTER EVIE ASKS. "YOU LOOK like crap. Also, why are you covered in wine? Never mind, you're always covered in alcohol. Here." She throws a kitchen towel at me and I use it to pat down my hair.

Evie comes back into the kitchen and tosses a T-shirt to me. It's one of mine. Evie lives in the apartment we grew up in on East 81st Street near Carl Schurz Park. I live on the West Side, but she likes the comfort of home. The apartment still has the same chintz couches, parquet floor, and white cracked walls that made up my childhood. The tiny galley kitchen forever emits the smell of coffee with lox and bagels and has the weak light of a small brick-wall-facing window. My first computer, an old Linux OS that I built myself, still sits in an honored place on the kitchen wall desk.

"So, why are you here? Existential crisis? Tired of living a meaningless existence and looking for change?" asks Evie.

She's only a year younger than me and she's ribbed me since birth. It's why I love her.

I drop into a chair at the kitchen table. "You could say that."

Evie opens the fridge and pulls out a container. She lifts the lid and reveals handmade linguini and red sauce. "I went to Francesco's today."

The corner of my mouth lifts. "How'd you know I'd be coming 'round?"

She knows that I'm a sucker for fresh pasta.

"I saw the announcement," she says in a more serious tone.

The clipping heats in my pocket.

"You have to stop punishing yourself," she says.

"Punishing myself?" I shake my head. "I've spent five years throwing parties, dating beautiful women and—"

"Exactly. You *hate* that stuff. You've been punishing yourself ever since Louisa the Loathsome left you and Garrett the Gross screwed you over."

"I don't hate that stuff."

She snorts.

"Fine. I hate it." I take a bite of the linguini. "This is really good."

Evie rolls her eyes. "You are such an idiot."

I take a minute to enjoy sitting in my childhood kitchen, in my old wooden chair, eating my favorite meal. This is the one place in the world where I can be me. My sister, my parents, they are the only people in the world who have seen through the outside to who I am.

"I miss you," says Evie.

"I'm right here." I take another bite of the pasta.

She sits down across from me and leans forward. "I mean I miss Sam. My brother. The one that used to build computers with me, and beat me at Trivial Pursuit and read Isaac Asimov."

I shake my head, denying what she's saying. No one liked

that version of Sam. Not the kids in school, not the people in the business world, not the media, not my ex-wife.

"You're the only one," I say. Then I remember the feeling I've been having lately, and I realize I miss myself too.

"Louisa and Garrett are two crappy people," Evie says. "And what they did is unforgivable."

Louisa was my college sweetheart and then wife. Garrett was my roommate and best friend then business partner. All the while I was working on my first business, BioTech, Garrett and Louisa were in bed together, literally and figuratively. After we became successful beyond our wildest imaginations Louisa left me for Garrett. She received BioTech in the divorce settlement. What struck hardest, though, was what Louisa said to me after I found out about her cheating. She'd said, "Why would you ever think that I love you? Look at you. A boring computer nerd with zero personality. You're so naïve. All anyone will ever want you for is your money. You don't have anything else to recommend you."

I learned the lesson that everyone had been trying to teach me since I was a kid. I was bullied for being smart. I was cheated on and left for loving computers and programming. So I embraced it. Entered into relationships with my eyes wide open. I made sure to make it clear to women that I dated them for their looks and they dated me for my money. Nothing more. No emotional connection and no intimacy. Because if I asked them to want me for me, if I believed they wanted me for me, I'd be disappointed. And if I fell in love and thought they loved me too only to find out otherwise...again...I'd be done.

"It's in the past," I say. "I've practically forgotten them."

Evie stands and grabs a fork from the kitchen cabinet. Then she sits down again and twirls up a forkful of the linguine. With her mouth full of pasta, she says, "Bull crap."

I grab another bite. Once Evie starts in on linguini it's gone in seconds.

She leans forward and jabs her fork at me. "What you need is to get out of the city, go somewhere where no one knows you. You can be yourself. Start building another business. Make friends. Maybe get a girlfriend who isn't obsessed with your net worth or your looks. Gag me."

I snort. "She'd have to be blind or in a media blackout to not recognize me."

"Don't be big-headed."

I hold out my hands and gesture to myself.

She sighs. "Fine. You're right. Unfortunately, your playboy alter ego *Frederick Knight* is a favorite of the news outlets."

"I *am* Frederick Knight," I say.

"Dad's Fred, you're Sam."

I look at the ceiling. Technically, I'm Fred Junior, but my friends and family have called me by my middle name since I was born. So, I'm Sam to my friends and Frederick to everyone else.

"Besides, Frederick is the persona you built to work through Louisa and Garrett stealing your company and breaking your heart. It's not you."

"Thank you, Shrink Evie."

"You realize I *do* have a master's degree in psychology."

"You realize therapists are more screwed up than their clients? And that they became shrinks so they can project their issues onto others and work out their problems vicariously through their clients."

She waves my statement away. "Anyway. I solved your problem."

I push aside the now empty container of linguini and lean back in my chair.

"How's that?" I ask. Evie always has a scheme or solution for other people's problems. She's a fixer and a meddler.

"I bought you a mansion."

"What?" I sit up.

"With your money, of course. Remember that account you gave me access to and told me I could do what I wanted with it? I did. I bought you a mansion."

"What are you talking about?"

"It's perfect." She sits up straight and grins. And not for the last time, I remember that her solutions rarely work out. She continues and I watch as her excitement grows. "It's an old stone mansion outside this adorable little town a couple of hours upstate. It's called Romeo, and it's the official town of love or something like that, and they have festivals, and a cute main street with flowers and a little footbridge over a river and stone sidewalks and a bakery and a bookshop and here's the best part...it's like in its own dimension or something. People there are really friendly, they all wave to each other and chat even with strangers, and they all believe in true love and soul mates and crap like that. But I don't think any of them keep up with the media, or the news, or the entertainment industry. It's another universe, I swear. You could go there and just be yourself. Just be you." She stops and looks at me and I realize really how worried she's been for me. "You could be you again."

There's a dull pain in my chest.

"Evie..."

"Don't say no. You've been wanting to start another business. Use this place as your springboard. Five years is too long. I think that birth announcement was a good thing. It's the kick in the pants you need to move on. Mom and Dad agree."

"You called them?" I ask.

She shrugs, but she looks embarrassed. She brought out the big guns. Mom and Dad are on a year-long African safari, living out their retirement dreams. Evie must've been really worried about me to talk to our parents about this.

"They want you to be happy," she says.

"I'm thirty-three years old, Evie. I don't need you to fix my life."

"I know. I'm sorry."

I look down at the kitchen table. Next to my hand is a black scorch mark. It's a burn from when I was an eleven-year-old kid soldering some of my first electronics. A lump grows in my throat. I still remember the secure feeling of sitting at the kitchen table, tinkering with computer parts while my mom made meatloaf and mashed potatoes for dinner.

"I guess I do need to get away," I say.

Evie lets out a cheer. Then she jumps up and gives me a hug.

"Idiot," I say, and the word is full of love for my meddling sister.

"Well, that'll teach you to give me access to a million-dollar bank account."

Or not. I have too much money as it is. After I lost BioTech, I sold my other business, a domain registration company, for eight hundred million dollars. With smart investments, the amount has only grown.

"You really don't like my public persona?" I ask.

"I hate it. I know you wanted kids with Louisa."

I send her a sharp look. We don't talk about that. I told her years ago in a moment of weakness.

She continues, "But you'll never have that if you keep playing the jerk-off playboy. No decent woman will look at you twice."

I think about the five years of trying to protect myself from hurt and trying to prove Louisa wrong. I basically proved her right. I only dated women that cared about status and money. And I made myself into a spectacle.

"You're right." I come to a decision. I'll go to Evie's town, check out the house she bought, and I'll get myself back on track. She's right, it's time I started working again.

I'm not interested in opening myself up or letting another woman hurt me, but I can stop playing the dissipated billionaire.

I can do that.

But as for a woman. No. I'm not going to open myself up for a world of hurt. Not ever again.

Not even if the woman was blind and had never heard of Frederick Knight.

3

VERONICA

THERE'S a man ahead on the trail. I scowl at his back. Every so often I catch sight of him. He's a couple hundred yards up, and when the curves of the trail straighten into a long stretch I watch him. He doesn't know I'm behind him. Why would he? He moves like an elephant. He breaks dry twigs, crashes through leaf piles, and makes more noise than a three-year-old in a candy factory. Clearly he's not an outdoorsman. I snort as he trips over a root and catches himself just in time.

It's barely seven in the morning. The crisp woodsy air and the golden morning light fill me with happiness. I take a breath and the sharp pine smell tickles my nose. Everything is perfect, at least it would be if the quiet weren't disturbed by the guy up ahead. He steps on another twig and the loud crack reverberating through the woods sends a jay squawking into the sky.

I expect he'll turn around soon. We're three miles from the trailhead, but it doesn't look like he has any gear with him. He's in shorts, a T-shirt, hat, and tennis shoes. But he doesn't have a pack or water that I can see. Not even the greenest day hiker would go much farther without any water. It's supposed to get hot today. I roll my shoulders and smile at the comforting weight of my frame pack. Chloe always teases me about my prepper tendencies and my obsession for all things survivalist. I'm not going to deny it, I love getting out on the trail, or into the backwoods and losing myself in the wild for a week or two.

I started in my teens. It was a rough time in my life. My mom and dad fought constantly, I felt so lost. Hiking, climbing, camping, those things saved my life. Now, even though I don't need them anymore to help me survive, they still make me feel strong and safe.

The man on the trail ahead turns to the west and starts into the woods. I look to the sky and shake my head. What the heck is he doing? He jumps over a large fallen tree trunk covered in moss and moves into the thick vegetation of the woods. This is survival no-no number one. Every year inexperienced hikers leave a trail and become lost in the woods. Some even die, sometimes only a hundred meters from the trail, because they've gotten turned around and they can't find their way back and they don't know how to survive off the land.

I pick up my pace and come to the place where the man left the trail. I can see him picking his way through the brush. He looks like he's just enjoying the day, meandering, and...oh no.

I curse as he steps into the mouth of a cave. There are plenty of caves in Upstate, dozens of them in the forests around Romeo. I steer clear of them.

"I'm not going after him," I say out loud.

There's a chattering of birds in the distance. I swat a mosquito that thinks it's a nice time to bite. I glare at the entrance to the cave. It's about five feet high and three feet wide. Ivy covers most of the opening. It's barely noticeable from the trail. If I remember right, this cave was discovered by school kids about one hundred and fifty years ago. This one hasn't been explored too much. To be honest, caves really aren't my thing. I tap my foot, expecting the man to come out of the cave any second.

But he doesn't.

I smack another mosquito. The forest is quiet. Now that the hiker isn't crashing through the trail making noise, the animals have started to come out again. I hear the steps of a careful deer, the chiding kuk-kuk-kuk of a squirrel, the liquid notes of a jay. The sounds paint the forest green and gold and beautiful.

But he still hasn't come out.

I roll my shoulders and the weight of my pack shifts. Inside my pack I have two weeks of provisions, a water filter and bottle, my canister stove and cook kit, a hatchet and multitool, my tent, sleeping bag, compass, maps, my first-aid bag, extra socks, needle and thread, light, duct tape, a whistle and mirror, there's more...needless to say, I'm well prepared for two weeks on my own in the woods. This is a light trip for me, I've gone six months on my own for a thru-hike.

I give him another minute, but still no movement. The guy might not realize it, but caves can be dangerous. They aren't something you should go and poke around in on your own.

But maybe he's actually really experienced? Maybe he's a caver, or a speleologist and he'll be annoyed that I'm coming after him.

Or maybe he's a criminal and he's going to check on the money from his last bank heist, or he's got his victims stored in the cave or...

Ugh.

A mosquito buzzes at my ear and I smack it.

I can't just walk away. I'll always wonder if the noisy hiker with no gear made it out okay. And if he doesn't...I'll blame myself.

"I'm going to have to go after him," I say.

I let out a sigh and then step off the trail.

Sure, he could be a creepy insane wackadoo, but he could also be a normal guy, probably from the city, who doesn't know the end of a stick from his...ahem.

My pack slaps against my back as I scramble over downed trees, a dry creek bed and thick foliage on my way to the cave. The smell of damp, limestone-scented air hits me as I come to the entrance and push away the vines.

"Hello?" I call.

My voice echoes, "lo, lo, lo."

I shiver. The cool damp air, probably about fifty degrees, fans over me. Shafts of light shift through the vines and dimly illuminate the interior. The cave mouth opens into a rounded chamber of rough limestone that narrows into a downward sloping passage.

I take out my flashlight and shine it onto the pale dirt. I can see footprints in the dirt leading to the passage.

I let out a long sigh and step into the cave. I won't go far. I've never explored a cave before. The darkness, their unknown nature, they give me the creeps. Sort of like when you're a kid at night and you're terrified of what might be under the bed or in the closet, that's what a cave feels like to me. They are nothing like the wide open freedom of a forest.

I shine my light toward the passage and step in the narrow confines. I press my hand against the rock wall. It's damp and cold. I let out a shaky exhale.

"Hello?" I call again.

No answer.

After about fifty feet of a slow descent I decide it's time to turn around. The darkness is heavier and the air is closed and stagnant. The only noise is the slow drip of water leaking from the ceiling building the mounded stalagmites rising from the ground and pulling down the stalactites dropping from the ceiling like sharks' teeth. I duck under another stalactite and see that I've come upon another chamber. The passage opens and I shine my light over glittering crystalline structures.

"Wow," I breathe.

The room sparkles in the beam of my flashlight and I'm mesmerized by the otherworldly beauty. The cavern is made of milky white stone twisted around like pulled taffy and tall spires that shine like diamonds rising to a ceiling of glittering, winking stars. No, not stars, crystals.

"Hello?" I call.

My voice echoes, again and again, until a symphony of hellos returns to me. I feel as if I'm in a cathedral, an underground cathedral, more beautiful than anything I've ever seen.

With my head tilted up and my eyes traveling up the spires to the glittering ceiling I step into the chamber. I step forward, once, twice, and again. Then my foot lands...on nothing. There's no ground in front of me.

My arms pinwheel. My heavy pack throws me off balance.

I cry out and fling my arms, trying to grab something, anything. My flashlight flies from my hands and drops into the pit. I plunge forward. As I do, I close my eyes. Certain that I'm about to die.

Then, there's a jerk and my arms yank back. My body twists and hits the slick wall of the crevice. My pack, the metal frame caught on something, a stalagmite, I think. I hang by my arms, suspended over black, open air. I kick my feet, claw at the wet rocky wall. If I can just get a handhold, a foothold, anything. Suddenly, there's a cracking noise, another jerk, I'm thrust forward and my arms wrench free from my pack.

I scream. There's nothing but black, open air beneath me.

As I start to fall, the second when I'm certain this is *the end*, someone grabs my arm.

I slam back against the wall. I'm hanging over the edge, and a stranger's grip is the only thing keeping me from plunging into the darkness. My heart punches painfully against my chest.

"Hold on." It's a man. His voice is deep and strained.

His grip is tight and painful and I'm so thankful for the burn of his bruising grasp.

"Help," I gasp. I look down. I can't see the bottom, it's a dark pit.

"Got you," he says.

Then he starts to pull me back up and I think, my word, it's the hiker and he's strong and he has me and he's going to save my life.

Then, the thought cuts short, because there's a strange groaning noise coming from the rock beneath me, a rumble. And then the edge of the wall breaks away, the man slides forward, pitches over me into open air and then we're both falling.

I grip his hand. We roll in the air and our limbs tangle together. Then a second later, a minute later, my mind can't tell, we hit bottom. My head slams against rock. There's blinding pain and a flash of light and a loud whooshing noise cracks through my skull. I try to fight past the pain and the lights sweeping in my eyes, but I can't.

My fingers loosen, feel like jelly, I drop the man's hand. For some reason everything feels wet and cold and like I'm floating. In fact, I think I am. I'm floating. And the man's next to me but I can't see him, it's too dark. I can only feel him.

"Are you okay?" I ask him. My voice sounds slurred and far away. He doesn't answer. I really hope he's okay. Then I lose the thought and sink into blackness.

4

SAM

I KICK MY LEGS, fighting to pull the woman to the surface. I have a hold of her beneath her arms. She's a dead weight and I pray that she's okay, that she didn't get hurt in the fall. The icy water urges me to kick harder. There's no light. I can't tell up from down. I'm going on pure instinct, and a prayer, please God, let me be swimming toward air.

I kick harder. My heart pounds in my ears and my lungs ache. Maybe I chose the wrong direction. Up was down, or down was up and I'm swimming to the bottom of the water. I start to panic. Then, just when I'm about to turn around, reverse direction, we break the surface. I gasp, drag in a harsh breath then cough and sputter. I draw the woman's head higher. Float on my back and hold her against my chest. She coughs and sputters.

Then, "Are you okay?" she asks. Her voice is ragged and soft.

Before I can answer, her head falls again to my chest and her body goes limp.

My blood goes cold.

"I'm okay. Are you alright?"

She doesn't answer, she lies heavy and still against me. I kick my legs to keep us at the surface and feel for her pulse. I let out a sigh of relief, it's strong and steady. At least there's that. She shivers and I'm reminded of how cold the water is. Like an ice bath. We're going to get hypothermia if I don't get us out of it soon.

But I can't see. There's no light. I dropped my phone when I went to grab her. I saw her flashlight fly from her grasp. Then I remember my watch. It's a waterproof divers watch, a twenty-thousand-dollar piece that Evie bought me last year for my birthday. She laughed because she said she'd spent my money to get it. I've worn it ever since. Thank the Lord. I press a button on the side and the display glows. It gives a dim light that barely illuminates the space around my hand. I hold up my arm and twist the watch in the air. The light catches on the white stone and reflects around the cavern. The water that was black in the pitch dark is turquoise and clear where the light hits. There. About twenty feet away I can just make out what looks like water hitting rock. I can't be sure. The light is too dim. But I swim that way because right now it's our best chance.

I'm breathing hard and shivering harder by the time I reach the rock wall.

"We made it," I tell the woman. I lift her onto the rock first, roll her onto the surface and then I climb out after her. Water sluices onto the rock and runs around us. It's cold. It's too cold. I feel for the woman's pulse. It's still strong, but her skin is like ice and she's shaking.

"You'll be okay," I say. I keep talking, because it's so dark and quiet in here that any voice, even my own, is better than the silence. "I've never been so scared as when I saw you fall," I tell her. I keep my voice low and soothing. I don't know how we're going to get out of here. Or even if there *is* a way out.

My phone is gone, hers is likely in her pack which is still up on the stalagmite at the top of the crevice. To be sure I pat her pockets. Carefully. I don't want her waking up thinking I'm some creep taking advantage. Nothing. They're empty. Not that a phone could get reception down in the depths of a cave.

"We'll get out of here," I tell her. I put my hand on her arm. Dang, she's cold. "I'll get you out of here. I promise."

I hear a scratching noise and then a rhythmic crunch, crunch, scratch. The hair on the back of my neck stands up. There's something else here with us.

I hit the display of my watch and look around. Nothing. I can't see anything. I hold it over the woman. I can barely make out the shape of her face.

She shivers again and I make a decision. I have to get her warm and I have to get her to help. I think the most urgent thing right now is getting warm.

But how?

Body heat. But first we need out of these soaking wet clothes.

"Dang it."

I kick off my shoes and socks and then pull off my T-shirt. I wring the water out of them and set them out on the rock. Then, I strip down to my boxers and wring out my shorts. I'm too cold to feel awkward. I jump up and down and rub my hands over my clammy skin. Then I kneel down next to the woman.

I untie and pull off her hiking boots and socks. Then I work the soaking wet long-sleeved shirt over her head. I wring it out and put it next to her socks and boots. I feel around in the dark for the buttons to her pants. The skin of her stomach is cold and taut.

I find the button.

Suddenly, her hand lashes out and grabs my throat. She squeezes and I freeze.

"Take off my pants and I'll kill you and leave your body in the dark."

I can't see her. I can only feel her freezing cold fingers pressing into my Adam's apple. I swallow.

"You're awake," I say. "Thank God."

Her fingers shake and relax on my throat.

"Are you okay?" I ask.

"What are you doing?"

I take her wrist and move her hand from my throat. "When we fell we landed in water. It was forty degrees at most. I'm worried about hypothermia. I was getting our clothes off so they can dry. I'm not..." I clear my throat.

I hear her moving over the rocks and dirt as she pushes herself up into a sitting position.

"Are you hurt?" she asks. Then even though we're not touching I feel her shiver violently.

"No. I'm fine."

She shivers again.

"Dang it, you're right," she says. I hear her zipper and she kicks off her pants. I grab them and wring the water from them. They're the quick-dry kind of material hikers like to wear so I think they'll dry fast. I lay them next to the other clothes.

"What's your name?" she asks.

"Sam," I say automatically. Usually I introduce myself as Frederick to strangers. Frederick Knight. But this situation is different. I don't want to be Frederick Knight down here. Not in this dark cave, freezing, cut off from civilization and possibly without a way out.

"I'm Veronica," she says. "Figured we should introduce ourselves before we do the horizontal tango."

I cough and sputter. "Ahh, what?"

"Kidding. Don't they always have sex in the movies to ward off hypothermia?"

"Right." I swallow.

"Seriously. Come here. My head hurts like a son of a gun and I'm freezing."

I feel the ground and move across the damp rock. When I touch her arm she lets out a long sigh. It does feel good. She's cold. So am I. But where our skin touches there's a warm thrum that makes me want to press every inch of our bodies together.

"Feels better," she says. "Do you mind?" She inches closer and presses her side to mine.

"No. That's good," I say.

I sit for a moment and enjoy the warmth between us, but then she shivers again.

"Screw this. Come here." I open my arms and legs, and even though she can't see, she can hear. She moves in between my legs and leans her back against my chest. I wrap my arms and legs around her and start to rub my hands over her skin. Then I rub my hands briskly together to create heated friction and run them over her again.

She burrows against me and lets out a sigh.

"Thank you," she says against my chest and the heat of her breath and her body warms me.

"Of course," I say and I keep running my hands over her.

After a while her skin warms and her shivers become less violent and more muted. When they do she shifts around and rubs her hands together. Then she moves them over my arms and my chest. Her hands are delicate, her fingers are long and thin with calluses at the tips. I shiver as she drags her hands down my chest.

"Cold?" she asks.

I nod, even though I know she can't see me. I don't think I can speak. She keeps creating warmth between her palms and then running her hands down my arms, my chest, my legs. I can't see anything. Which is the only explanation I have for why I find her touch the most erotic thing I've ever felt in my life. I don't know where her fingers are going to land next. And because I can't see anything, my other senses are completely focused on her. The rhythm of her breath and the whisper of her shifting movements against the rock. The heat of her hands dragging over me and sending warmth coursing through me. Everywhere she touches, heat spreads. Her hands move up my legs, my thighs... I stop her progress by placing my hands over hers. She stills. Then I draw her in close and wrap her against me. My breath is harsh in the quiet.

She relaxes and leans into me. Her hair, damp now rather than soaking wet, fans out over my chest as she presses her cheek into my shoulder.

"Don't worry," I say.

She shifts in my arms then pulls away. I feel cold when she moves away, and it's not just from the lack of body heat.

"My clothes are dry," she says. I hear the fabric rustling as she gets dressed. I stand and pull on my shorts and shirt. They're still damp and cold and feel uncomfortably clammy. I fold my socks and put them in my pocket, then slip on my shoes.

"Do you have a light?" she asks.

"My watch," I say. I press the button and the low glow gives its dull illumination. I can see the outline of her. She's about six inches shorter than me and athletic. I can't tell she's athletic from the light, I know that from the feel of her in my arms. And that's all I know about what she looks like. I raise my arm and turn the display so that the light can reflect off the walls. Some of the white crystals catch and spark.

"I don't remember...which way did we come from?" she asks.

I walk to the edge of the rocky shore. "Here," I say. The water glows clear blue under the light. "We fell from up there. I swam us to shore."

She lets out a long sigh.

"From what I could tell," I say, "we fell thirty, maybe forty feet before we hit the pool. I don't think we'll be able to get back out that way."

She walks to the edge of the water. I hold out my watch and try to illuminate the pool and the walls. I think we're in a large dome. The walls slope up in a sharp curve and are full of twisted stone and spiked mounds. Somewhere in the ceiling of the dome, thirty or so feet above us, is the hole we fell through. It's too dark to see where it is. The only thing I can tell is we aren't getting out of here by going back up.

I hear rustling and turn to Veronica. She starts to pull off her boots.

"I'm gonna try. I'll wade in, locate a route. Climb out, get help."

I'm dumbstruck. "Do you see the wall? It curves like the inside of a sphere. You'd have to be Spiderman to climb that. Look at the condensation on the stones, they're slicker than ice. And what happens when you fall? What if you're hurt and I can't find you?" The thought of her lost in the black water sends a chill through me. "It's not climbable."

She paces the edge of the water and peers into the blackness and up into the dark. Finally she stops.

"You're right," she says. Her voice breaks a bit, but then she turns and walks back toward our resting spot. I follow, breathing a sigh of relief. The only thing that would've come from attempting to climb the wall was injury or worse.

"Do you have any outdoors experience? Caving? Hiking? Anything?" she asks.

"My parents took me camping when I was eight," I say. "We

went on this trippy cave tour that dumped into a gift shop." I hear her sigh. "No. No experience."

"Why'd you go in this cave? What were you thinking?" she asks. She sounds angry.

"Hey. Why'd you? If you remember correctly, I was trying to save you."

"No. I was trying to save you. I saw you from the trail. I wanted to make sure you didn't get hurt so I came after you."

"Oh. Right." I clench my hands, I shouldn't have come in the cave. There was something about it that drew me in, but I should've kept walking. "You're from around here?" I ask.

"I live nearby. I hike and camp along this trail nearly every weekend."

"Then you know how to get out?"

She's quiet. I know her answer before she says it.

"No."

"What does that mean?" I ask, although I can already make an educated guess.

"It means we can stay here and wait for someone to find us. It's not likely they will, though. Did you tell anyone where you'd be today?"

I want to kick myself. "No. No one knows where I am." I was just going out for a short walk. I'd driven up from New York City this morning and wanted to stretch my legs and explore the woods around the new house. "No one will miss me. Not for a day or two at least."

She lets out a long breath. "Me either. I mean, my friends know I'm hiking, but they're used to not hearing from me for days."

"We could stay here and wait, see if someone comes in, or if rescuers find us," I say, thinking the situation through. A sense of doom closes around me.

"It would make sense to stay and wait for rescue. That's usually the wisest course of action," she says.

"Do you have food?" I ask.

"No. Do you? Water?"

"No."

"Everything was in my pack," she says. Her voice is full of recrimination.

"It's alright," I say. I point to the passage a few feet from where we stand. "That might be the way out."

"Or the way deeper," she says.

We're silent for a moment and the enormity of the situation hits. It'll take days for anyone to notice we're missing, Evie might get worried after two or three days of no contact, but not any sooner than that. Then, it will take days more for rescuers to search the vast woods of the area, and it's unlikely they'll think to look in a cave a hundred yards off the trail. It could be weeks before we're found, if ever. And we have no food. We could starve to death sitting here waiting for someone to find us.

Veronica starts to pace. "Eighty percent of survival is a mental game. We got this. The pool water probably isn't clean, but we can drink the water drops coming off the stalactites. We can huddle together for warmth. But we have to decide, do we wait here or do we take the passage and try to find a way out?"

"Do many people come in this cave? A random hiker? Kids? Is there any chance of that happening?"

"It's not likely. Two or three people hike this section of the trail per week. I'm one of them. The chances are close to nil that anyone will come looking in here."

It seems pretty clear what we have to do.

"Let's find a way out," I say. Although my voice sounds firm, the sense of doom presses harder. "The entrance is probably only forty feet down this tunnel."

"Right. Exactly. Let's go then," she says.

I pause. Wait for her to move.

"Hold my hand," she says.

I do. I thread her fingers through mine. I hear her let out a low sigh.

"Thank you," she whispers.

I squeeze her hand. "You're welcome."

Then we step into the low, tight confines of the dark tunnel.

Forty feet later we make it, not to an exit, but to a choice.

Left or right.

5

VERONICA

LIFE DEFINITELY KNOWS how to throw twists and turns. This morning I was running from the idea of my soul mate coming to town, now I'm just praying that I make it out of this cave alive. I want to get back to my friends, be there for the birth of my goddaughter.

I couldn't care less about Frederick Knight.

I look over at the soft glow of blue light surrounding Sam. I wonder for a second if fate pulled a number on me and knocked me into this cave with my soul mate, but the man I'm with isn't Frederick Knight. This man's name is Sam and you can learn a lot about someone when put in a survival situation. So far I know he's level-headed, he risks himself for others, and although he was reckless coming into the cave, he doesn't strike me as someone who is careless. He seems decent and I think...I can trust him. I know I can. He saved me. Pulled me from the water when I passed out and kept me from hypothermia. My motto has always been love makes you weak. I usually extend that to not depending on men. Because they're all players or wanna-be players—ad nauseam. Except...none of that seems to apply here. Nothing in my past relates to a situation where I'm lost in a dark cave with a man I don't know and have to depend on. And who doesn't seem like a player or a wanna-be player at all.

"There's a draft coming from the right," he says. He holds his hand in front of the tunnel entrance.

I feel it too. A slight pulling of air up and away from us. I don't know whether that means it leads to an exit or farther into the cave. I think I remember some cavers telling me that it could be either, that drafts aren't a reliable indicator of an exit. Cavers love to sit around drinking beer and reminiscing about caving. I sometimes run into them on my longer hikes. Right now, I'm wishing I paid more attention.

"I think..." I pause. "Can you hold your light over the ground? Look to see if there are any signs of humans or animals coming through before us?"

"Good thought."

He squats down and holds his watch over the ground. I bend down and scan the earth as he moves the light over the dirt and rocks. The only sign of life is our own footprints. No other markings. No rubble, or grooves, or tracks, or anything. Nothing to guide our decision.

"Well, there goes that thought." I squint at the ground. The cave is mostly limestone, a dull yellowish tinged white. The ground is a mix of dirt, some loose rocks, and solid stone. Already, everything looks the same. It will be so easy to get turned around in here. I bend and grab some of the smaller stones.

"I'm going to make a cairn. I don't want to get turned around." I start stacking the rocks at the entrance to the tunnel on the right.

"Right. I'll make an arrow pointing back the way we came."

We take a minute to stack a noticeable cairn, and a rock

arrow pointing back to the pool. When we're finished I stand and smack the dirt from my hands.

We decide that we should leave something at the pool in case rescuers rappel down. After a quick hike back and a discussion we leave a rock message stating Sam and Veronica, the date, and an arrow pointing the way we went.

Back at the fork we take the tunnel to the right. Sam leads. Before long we're both stooped over and using our hands along the walls to pull us through the tight confines. The wet rock is cold and slimy and my hands slip over the stone. The air smells strongly of mineral, like you've held up a handful of gravel after a rainstorm and stuck your nose in it. Every so often, the soft glow of Sam's watch hits a stalactite and it looks like a face, or an animal, or in one case, a fried egg. The only noise is the scrape and the echo of my boots and his shoes against the ground and our labored breathing.

This tunnel feels as tight and confined as a stone coffin.

The thought scrapes down my skin and lifts the hairs on my arms.

"Talk to me," I say.

Sam stops and I pull up short behind him.

"What?"

I shake my head. "I don't..." I pause, "I think it'll be easier if we talk."

"Alright."

I pull in the mineral-tinged air. "Let's make an agreement," I say. "Nothing's off limits. We can say anything. No judgments. Talk about anything we want. And then, if we ever make it out... I mean, when we make it out, what we said stays in the cave."

"You have a lot of secrets?" he asks, and I hear the smile in his voice.

"No," I say. I shrug. "I just don't want to, okay I don't think we're going to die, but if we do, I don't want to be with a stranger when I do. I want...I'd like to be with someone I know and trust. Someone I like. So..."

"I'm a computer geek," he says suddenly.

And he says it in such a way that I start to laugh. "What?"

"I love computers. Programming, app development, the beauty of a perfect line of code. I used to sit in front of a computer for hours on end and go so deep in the code that I forgot to eat. Forgot the time and whether it was day or night."

"Wow," I say. "That's pretty awesome."

"It's...what?"

He sounds surprised. I can just make out his head turning quickly back to me.

"It's awesome that you love something so much. Lots of people don't have that."

He's quiet for a moment, then, "You're right." Again he sounds surprised.

Then he starts moving forward again. I follow after him. He keeps talking, his voice echoing back to me and filling the darkness.

"I let some people convince me otherwise."

"Who's that?"

"Nobody." He pauses. "That's not true. No secrets, right?"

"Exactly," I say. I stoop lower. My breaths grow shorter. I'm not naturally claustrophobic, but the walls closing in are starting to get to me.

"We're going to have to crawl here," Sam says. I hear him lowering to the earth. I drop down onto all fours and crawl forward. Suddenly, I feel tears at the corners of my eyes. We crawl forward and all I want to do is turn around. What if the ceiling caves in, we'll be trapped, we'll die in this rocky coffin. A tear slides down my cheek.

"Who was it?" I ask desperately. "Who made you believe that?" I need to hear his voice.

"I don't remember when it started. I guess at school. I was awkward intelligent, not the kind that teachers like or kids admire, but the uncomfortable, socially unacceptable kind."

"What does that mean?"

"The kind where you don't fit. By the time I was eight I was reading college textbooks and building my first computer. I was bored in school and teachers didn't know what to do with me. I got terrible grades and was labeled a troubled student. My parents didn't understand how I could understand books on quantum computing and build databases but barely pass third grade."

"It's because you hated it."

"I hated it."

I follow his slow pace through the tunnel and keep moving forward, following the sound of his voice.

"So you were picked on."

"You could say that."

I can tell from the guarded sound of his voice that he was more than picked on.

"I wasn't good at sports. I wasn't good-looking. I was painfully shy. Just picture the stereotypical Brainiac in teen movies and you have me pegged."

I have a picture of him in my mind now. He probably wears glasses for reading and working on the computer. I bet he doesn't care about fashion or keep up with trends. He has a confident voice so I think he's not bad-looking, but also not gorgeous like...ugh, Frederick Knight. No, I bet Sam has a pleasantly average face. With intelligent eyes and a steady expression. I like the picture I have of him.

"You weren't bitter though. Or spiteful," I say. I get the feeling that it may have hurt at the time, but he's long over it.

He laughs. "No. I was too busy working on my programming ideas to be bitter."

"So who made you ashamed of flying your freak flag?"

He snorts. "Do you have a freak flag?"

"Obviously. I have a two-year supply of food and resources all ready for the apocalypse. It's all in my DIY fallout shelter. Man, if only I had a tenth of those supplies right now."

"That's incredible."

"We're not talking about me," I say. "Who was it?"

"Me."

"What?"

"It was me. Nobody can make you believe anything without your consent. I chose to believe it."

I'm so surprised that I stop crawling for a moment. I've never known anyone to so calmly state that fact.

I pull myself over a rough section of rock. The tunnel is only about two and a half feet tall now. I'm not sure we could turn around it we wanted to. If this dead ends we'll have to back out.

Sam grunts and I hear rock scraping. "It's tight here," he says. He kicks at the ground and keeps going. I hold my breath as I squeeze through the narrowing. Then, the tunnel opens up a bit and I'm able to stoop again instead of crawl.

"I got married in college."

"Yeah?" My voice is high, and I realize that I hadn't thought of him as married. It strikes me as wrong.

"Louisa. She was the first and only girl I dated before marriage. I didn't have any experience and I thought..."

"What?"

"I started a company with my roommate. He was my best friend. The company was successful. I developed the software, he sold and marketed it. We were on top of the world."

Oh no. I can see where this is going.

"But he and my wife had been sleeping together since before the wedding. I found out about the affair and they declined to stop. So, she got the company in the divorce settlement and I got my side business."

They were players. I feel anger for him.

I adjust my image of him. He's a comfortably average-looking, techy entrepreneur who is struggling to make a living after receiving a heavy blow.

"So...you stopped doing your computer thing?"

"You could say that."

"Because you believed she cheated on you because you were a computer prodigy?"

"Sounds pretty idiotic when you say it that way."

"I hope you know that whatever she said to you to blame you or make the affair look like your fault, none of it was true. When people have affairs they reach out and grab ahold of any excuse they can for what they did. Just as long as they don't have to say, *I did this*."

"So, are you telling me," he says, and there's another smile in his voice, "that she didn't cheat because I love computers and am a super geek?" I can feel the laughter coming off him.

"I guarantee it," I say.

"I like you," he says.

I grin, and the dark doesn't feel so scary.

"I like you, too," I say. I have to amend my statement from the other day. There are three types of men, players, wanna-be players, and good men. Like Sam.

Up ahead, there's the sound of rocks sliding, then Sam drops out from in front of me.

"Sam?" I call.

I hear him climb back up. I reach forward and feel the top of his shoulders. They're solid and muscular.

"It's another cavern," he says. There's excitement in his voice. He grabs my arms and pulls me down. I slide against his side and drop to my feet. I stay in his arms, pressed tightly against him. It feels good to stand and I don't want to step away from him. After so long crawling through that tunnel, separated by the dark, I need to feel the heat of him.

He squeezes me to his side and I hold him.

Then he lights his watch and holds it high.

"Oh...wow," I say.

It's unbelievable. It's...

"Is that the only way across?" I ask.

"I think so."

We both look at the edge of the light. It spreads from his watch in a weak beam and traces the white limestone.

"It's a bridge," I say.

He brings his hand down and pulls me closer. His arms tense around me and I can tell that he's worried. For me.

"I'm alright," I say.

It's a natural stone bridge, an arch that hangs above a dark chasm. If we want to keep going we have to cross it, an unknown, that extends beyond what we can see.

"We can turn around," he says. "Try the other fork."

"Alright. Yes, let's turn around." The metallic taste of panic is overwhelming.

He lifts me up and I start to scramble back up to the tunnel. But because of our previous passage, the displacement of rocks, or the echoing of my climb back up, something shifts the rocks in the tunnel. There's a loud crashing noise, a rumble that shakes the tunnel, then the whole thing collapses. Sam yanks me down right before a section of the roof falls. He drops to the ground and throws his body over mine. A rush of dust shoots out of the tunnel and gravel sprays over us.

Finally, the noise and dust settle.

"I don't think," I say, "that we're going back that way."

6

SAM

I PULL Veronica into my side. She's brave. One of the bravest people I've ever met. She hasn't shown an ounce of fear since we fell, she hasn't complained or lost her head, but I can tell that she's scared. She holds herself stiff against me and her breath comes out in short pants. I run my hands down her arms. Her skin is clammy. Of course, it can't be above fifty degrees in here. It isn't surprising that she's cold, my clothing's still damp and I'm feeling the chill.

I look at my watch. We've been in the cave for five hours. It's just past noon.

"I'm sorry I had us leave the pool," I say.

I knew before that we were in a serious situation, but it didn't truly sink in until now. We're trapped in this cave, and we can't go back, we can only go forward and pray that there's a way out. There's no way back to the pool or to the chance that someone will happen upon us.

"It's my fault," I say.

"Don't say that." She stiffens against me, then buries her hands in my shirt. I feel her shake her head. "You can't second-guess. We can't start doubting our decisions. Besides, *you* didn't have us leave...we made the choice together."

"You're right." There's nothing more to say about it. We won't survive by sitting here regretting our choices. Whether in a cave or in life you have to move forward. "How should we do this?" I ask.

We walk along the edge of the cavern. The ledge we're on extends twenty feet along the wall and five feet out over a deep hole. Veronica picks up a rock and drops it over the edge. I count slowly from zero to three before we hear the rock clatter at the bottom.

"Deep," she says.

"One hundred and eleven feet deep," I say.

"What? How do you know?"

"Newtonian physics. I modified the free fall equation to fit the specific environment and then..." I clear my throat. "It's one hundred eleven feet deep. Roughly."

She buries her face in my chest and her shoulders shake. I have a moment of panic until I realize that she isn't crying. She's laughing.

"I love how you just calculated how far we'll plunge to our deaths. *Roughly.*"

I smile. "You like that?" I ask.

She keeps laughing. "Absolutely. What other amazing things can you do?"

She tilts her face up to mine and although I can't see her, I can feel her warm breath and the nearness of her mouth.

"What do you want to know?" I ask.

She moves her hands to my shoulders. "If we get out of here, what will you do? What do you wish you'd done?"

Kiss you. The thought pops into my mind. I want to kiss her. She doesn't know who I am, how much I'm worth, or what I look like, but she likes me. And not the aloof, suave, billionaire me, but the me that I don't show anyone. The me that no one can see anymore.

"I'd start another business," I say. "I've been thinking about it for years. But I haven't done it."

"What kind of business?"

"I want to create a think tank with the mission of utilizing technology to aid humanity. It could be technology and ocean cleanup, or technology and clean energy, or technology and—"

"Search and rescue."

I smile. "Exactly. We could create a remote-controlled, video and GPS-enabled rover that finds people lost in caves. Forget about Mars exploration, we need rovers for caves."

"You should do it," Veronica says.

I squeeze her arms. "I will." Then I step back from her and turn to the bridge.

"What are the chances it collapses?" she asks.

"I don't know."

"Oh. I was hoping you had another equation."

She takes my hand and threads her fingers through mine. It's funny, in the outside world where there's light, touch isn't so necessary. But here, touch feels almost as vital as breathing. Without touch the sheer blackness and oppression of the cave start to pull you under. A warm hand, a voice, they're lifelines.

"There's an equation for load-bearing capacity, but I can't see the length of the bridge, or its width, or any of the other measurements I need."

"Oh. So it could break with us on it?"

"That's right."

She lets out a long breath. Then, "I guess we better get to it then."

"I can go first," I say. "Make sure it's safe. That way if it breaks only one of us will—"

"No way. I'm not going to sit up here on my own with your

dead butt at the bottom of that one-hundred-and-eleven-foot pit. Nope. We do this together." She squeezes my hand.

"Alright," I say. "We'll lay down on the rock, distribute our weight and crawl across."

"Like on thin ice," she says.

"Exactly. Stay behind me, at the light's edge."

"To distribute our weight."

"Right. We'll go slow."

We're at the beginning of the bridge. I start to bend down.

"Hang on," Veronica says.

"Yeah?"

She puts her hands on my shoulders, then to my face. Her fingers feather over my jaw, rubbing over my stubble. I still as I sense her tilting her face up. She drags her thumbs over my lips and then I feel her lips a millimeter from mine. Her breath teases my mouth and the air between us heats. My lips tingle and then she leans in presses her mouth to mine.

Neither of us move. Her hands still on my face. Our lips remain as quiet and as still as the darkness around us. Then I taste her, sweet and salty. I take her bottom lip and run my tongue over her. She opens her mouth and invites me in. Slowly, I explore her. I can't see her, so I paint her in my mind. Her lower lip is lush and full and wide. There's a dip in the middle and I circle my tongue around it. Then I move to her upper lip and trace the shape of it. I never understood why anyone would call someone's mouth bow-shaped until now. Her upper lip forms a perfect cupid's bow. My hands itch to touch her, so I bring them up to her cheeks and run them over the smoothness of her skin. Her cheeks are high and full, and as I run my fingers over her, tracing her features, I explore her mouth. She lets out a small groan and her teeth scrape my bottom lip. I run my thumbs over her eyebrows, the soft skin of her eyelids, and I play with her eyelashes. She sends her fingers over my jaw and into my hair. She grabs the ends and tugs, then pulls me closer. Then she takes my tongue into her mouth and sucks. There's no light in the cave, but sparks flicker and crackle like fireworks behind my closed eyelids.

I open my eyes, expecting to see the cavern light up. But there's no light. Only Veronica pulling away, leaving my lips tingling and the rest of me wanting more.

"That was…" I trail off.

"For good luck," she says. "Let's try not to die."

I swallow and the warm glow vanishes.

"Right."

"But if we do," she says, "it was really nice knowing you. You're making me rethink some of my theories on life."

"Oh yeah?"

I get down on my belly and start a slow crawl onto the bridge.

"Tell me about it," I say. I know she likes to hear a voice in the dark. So do I.

"How about this, I'll tell you if we make it across."

"Deal," I say.

I crawl forward slowly, keeping on my belly, scraping along the rock. I hold my breath for a moment, waiting for the bridge to crack. It holds. I breathe again. I hear Veronica drop down to the ground and begin to crawl after me. My heart pounds against the stone and my knees and shins scrape on the rock. They're cut up from the tunnel, and the rock of the bridge grinds into my raw skin. The sting of the rock abrading my skin centers me and I move forward. The blackness opens before me, and the dim blue light of my watch illuminates the way a few inches at a time.

"You know how you said that you're going to start your business when we get out of here?" Veronica asks.

"Yeah?"

"I'm going to go see my mom," she whispers.

I pull myself forward over a rough patch of rocks. A few stones fall and seconds later the crack of them hitting bottom echoes through the cavern.

"I haven't..." Veronica's voice shakes. We both ignore the next handful of rocks falling off the bridge. "I haven't spoken to her in ten years. I'm...I'm going to see her."

"What happened?" I ask.

The bridge starts to narrow and within a few feet, it's only three feet wide. Then two.

"It's narrow here. Twenty-four inches max. Be careful."

"I will."

I'm quiet as I concentrate on keeping on top of the bridge. As I crawl, more rocks slide off.

Behind me, I hear Veronica's slow crawl and labored breathing.

"You okay?" I ask.

"I'm good. I'm a rock climber, you know. You should worry about yourself. I've never seen such a flat-footed hiker."

I smile at her teasing tone. I may have been awkward and not into sports as a kid, but as an adult I lift, climb at the gym on the rock wall, run.

"What happened with your mom?" I ask.

"I was angry at her for not meeting my standards. I blamed her for not living the way I wanted her to. I only just figured that out. In this stupid cave. I stopped talking to her because I thought she'd ruined our lives by not walking away from my dad, that she was weak and...I wanted her to be stronger."

"Kids want their parents to be invulnerable. Not to have flaws. That's not anything to be ashamed of. It's normal."

"Yeah," she says in a small voice. "But I punished her for it. I cut her off. I'd like her to know that I love her. That even though I don't agree with her choices, I still love her."

"She knows," I say.

Then the glow of my watch illuminates the end of the bridge. "We made it," I say. "I can see the other side. There's a ledge and another passage."

"Thank you God."

The last few feet to the ledge seem to take hours. Waiting for Veronica to make it to the ledge seems even longer. When we're both off the bridge we move away from the wall.

We sit with our backs to the wall taking deep, slow breaths. My heart slows and the sting in my shins fades.

"Alright," I say, "It's time for you to share what theories on life you've changed."

She moves closer and presses her arm and legs against mine.

"I thought you'd forget."

"Not a chance."

She leans into me and draws her knees up. "I'll tell you as we take on the next tunnel?"

"Deal," I say.

We collect a few stones and make a cairn at the entrance to the tunnel then I lead the way in. This tunnel is about seven feet tall and five feet wide. I keep the dim glow of my watch lit and move carefully over the jutting rocks and stalagmites. We're getting thirsty, so every so often we stop at a dripping stalactite and try to catch drops of water. The water drizzles into my mouth and tastes strongly of limestone and minerals.

"I had a theory for most my life," Veronica says. "That there are two types of men."

"Am I going to like this theory?"

She laughs. "Doubtful. But you're the reason I've started rethinking things. You, well, and my best friend's husband, but mostly you...you're proving it wrong."

I turn back to her, but can't see anything but her outline.

"What's the theory?" I ask.

"That all men in the world are either players or wanna-be players. There's no other type."

Surprise hits me and I trip over a stalagmite and catch myself on the wall.

"Are you okay?" she asks. She's concerned for me. Dang it, of course she's concerned. She thinks I broke her theory of players and wanna-be players. Me. The King of Players.

"I'm...yeah. I'm good." I right myself and keep moving forward. "So, you, ah, changed your mind?"

"I did. Well, sort of. I mean, players and wanna-be players still exist. But, I mean, you're not...look at you, well don't look because it's pitch dark, you know what I mean, but look at you. You had only one girlfriend, your wife, and she cheated on you, and then you...you're decent and smart and...I was wrong. I admit it. It just took getting trapped down here with a good man to realize it. So, I'm probably going to have to amend my theory to make room for good men."

My watch light fades and the darkness pressing down on me feels strangely similar to guilt. There are no secrets here, that was our deal. She doesn't know who I am. I have to tell her.

"My theory started with my dad," she says. "He used to take me with him when I was little to help him pick up women. You know, the cute little girl, sad single dad routine. Except he and my mom were still married. But he didn't care. For years I watched him pick up women. I saw all his moves, learned it like a playbook. After he died, my mom and I found his little black book, it had almost a thousand names in it. I was there for nearly half of them."

My throat burns. I feel hurt for the child she was, that a father would do that. "I'm sorry," I say thickly. "That was..."

"Horrible of him. Super crappy. I know."

"It was wrong. I'm sorry." We're quiet for a moment, then, "Not all men are like that."

"Unfortunately, the men I dated were. I saw them use all the pick-up moves I knew so well. I saw it when they dated my friends, I saw it at bars, in movies. It seemed like they were everywhere. I never met a guy that could prove my theory wrong. Until you." She seems happy, almost pleased with her discovery. "I guess, if I get out of here, I should rethink my stance."

"Or stick with me," I say. Then I hear her stop walking and I realize that she's surprised. So am I. I didn't think before saying it, the words just came out.

"That's a thought," she says.

We start walking again. There's a short climb, a few natural stairs. I reach down to help but Veronica has already boosted herself up. A heavy weight is settling over me. I have to tell her.

"I didn't..." I stop.

"What?"

I clear my throat. "After I got divorced, I dated a lot of women."

"Okay?"

"I was trying to prove my ex-wife wrong. Or right. When she'd said no one would want me. I wanted to wipe away what she'd said, I..."

"You don't have to explain yourself. My best friend was cheated on, it took her a long time to feel that she was *worthy* again. If you had to go on a few dates to get there, that's your business."

"I mean it was a little more than a *few*."

She laughs. "Alright, fine. You can call yourself a player or a wanna-be player. But I don't think you *really* are."

"Thank you," I say. "You're right. I'm not."

"Good."

She reaches toward me and grabs my hand.

Another six hours pass. We come to forks and turns, and leave cairns and arrows every time we take a new route. It's lucky we do, because I've lost count of the number of dead ends. We turn around and try another route and another. The pressure of the darkness increases and every so often we hear noises. Scratching, thumping, rustling. But we never see any life. No sign of it. Just noises in the dark.

At eight o'clock we stop and drink as much water as we can stomach from a dripping stalactite. We're in a small room, about eight feet in circumference. It leads into a small passage. It looks like it'll be another crawl.

"Can we stop and rest?" Veronica asks.

"Good idea."

I find a clear dry area and brush away the bits of gravel and broken rock. I sit down and Veronica sits and leans into me. Over the past hours we've talked about everything and nothing. Her business, her friends, her soon-to-be born goddaughter, her fears and her ambitions, how much she loves small towns and the outdoors. I've told her about my childhood in the city, my family, where I've traveled, my worries and my goals. The more we talk, the faster time moves. I feel like I know her better than I've ever known anyone. I think if we do die, she has her wish. She won't die with a stranger, she'll have a friend.

I reach out and take her hand. She leans her head against my shoulder.

"We could try to sleep," I say.

"I don't know if I could."

I lean back to the ground. The cold of the rock seeps through my clothes. I take Veronica and pull her on top of me. "Here. I'm warmer."

She relaxes against me, puts her hands on my chest and rests her head on my shoulder. Warmth spreads between us and I start to think about the kiss we shared before the bridge. I wrap my arms around her back and pull her closer. I rest my head against hers and close my eyes.

After a few minutes of silence, when I think she's almost fallen asleep she shifts and lifts her head.

"It's funny," she says.

"What's that?"

"I was thinking about pick-up lines. The ones where the guy says, 'I feel like I've known you forever,' or 'no one understands me but you,' or 'I wanted you from the first day I knew you.' You know those lines?"

"Yeah. I do." I'd just been thinking them.

"I never thought I'd ever feel that way. That I'd know exactly what they're saying." She drops her head back to my shoulder. "Do you know what I mean?" she asks.

I feel her heart beat softly against my chest and the length of her along my body. She feels as if she belongs there, like we've lain like this a thousand nights before and we'll keep doing it far into the future. She fits me.

"I know exactly what you mean," I say.

If I didn't know better, I'd think we've known each other years instead of a day.

She nods and her fingers splay over my chest. "Funny thing, I was in the woods this morning because my best friend's aunt, she's psychic, predicted my soul mate. She's never wrong and she predicted the man I'm supposed to spend the rest of my life with."

A sharp pain hits me in the chest. I shift Veronica in my arms. "You were going to meet him?"

"Heck no. I was running. The guy's a sleaze. The worst sort of creep. You have no idea."

"I hate him," I say jokingly. But I do. I'm insanely jealous of a guy I've never met. Her supposed soul mate.

"You're nothing like him. He uses women like they're disposable. He's conceited. Arrogant. I'd rather sit in this cave for a decade than be with him."

"That bad?"

"Trust me. This guy is the epitome of a player. There's no way I'd ever be with him."

I smile. I'm starting to feel better. Clearly, there's no need to be jealous. Besides... "You realize psychics are scientifically improbable? So, you really don't need to worry."

She laughs into my chest. "Bless your heart. Miss Erma, the soul mate seer, has a record of success thicker than the Bible. She's been at this for decades and she's never been wrong."

Dang it. I'm back to being jealous of the player.

"Except, the joke's on Erma because it's likely we won't get out of here. So, no soul mate for me."

I don't like that. "Hey. You're the one who said survival is eighty percent mental. No more of that talk. I'll get you out of here." Even if it means delivering her to the conceited, egotistical player.

"I'll get *you* out of here," she says. I smile, because her confidence is back.

"Don't worry," she says. "I won't be with him. Not ever. I promise."

"Yeah?" I ask. I'm not sure why the answer means so much. Except, when she braces her hands on the ground and moves her mouth over mine I realize I actually do know why.

"Promise," she says. "I'd rather be right here with you than with him."

I don't like her mentioning *him*, because her breath hitches and her voice catches. So I lean up and kiss the sound of *him* from her lips and replace him with me.

7

SAM KISSES ME. His mouth is warm and gentle. He brushes his lips over mine, and when I kiss him back he makes a low growl in his throat. The noise sends a vibration through me and my body lights up. He starts to pull away, so I send my hands into his hair and pull his mouth back to mine.

"I wish we'd met out there," I say.

He takes my mouth again and sends his tongue over my lips. I shiver when he pulls back.

"Where? Tell me how you'd want us to meet," he says.

I draw my hands through his hair, over his forehead and down his nose. It's narrow and there's a bump at the end. I feel his lips with my fingertips. They're firm, but his bottom lip has the slightest pout. His jaw is hard and the stubble growing in tickles my fingers. I move my hands down his neck, I feel his pounding pulse and move to his shoulders. The muscles in them tense and I move my hands down his biceps.

"You're muscular for a computer geek," I say. "I wonder what you look like."

He grunts and pulls me down to his mouth again. I play with his bottom lip and enjoy the comfort of being in his arms.

When he pulls back from my mouth I draw my hands down his face and cup his jaw.

"I look like me," he says. "Tallish, short hair, hazel eyes."

I laugh and I realize it doesn't actually matter what he looks like. His appearance doesn't matter at all.

"Alright. Let me think," I say. I relax against him as his hands wander over my back, my arms, and draw a slow circle over my lower back. It's getting late and I'm tired, my head still hurts, I'm hungry, thirsty, and we might not make it out of here alive. But Sam's hands, circling slowly across my back, my ribs, my sides are making me feel safe and...loved.

Everywhere he touches fills with a sparkling liquid warmth that spreads until I feel like he and I are floating and there is nothing except us. I can't think of anything except the next place he's going to touch and the way my breasts have gone heavy against his chest and the place between my thighs is starting to ache. I can feel him growing hard beneath me. I shift until I'm centered over him and then I move my hips, just barely, so that I rub along his length.

He lets out a harsh breath and his hands still.

My word, I want him. I want him so much.

"We would meet one weekend on the White Pine Trail," I say. My voice sounds languid and huskier than usual.

"We would?"

I rock my hips against him and he hisses. A warm spark lights inside me and starts to burn.

"We wouldn't like each other at first," I say.

His fingers press into my hips and he pulls me closer. I rock against him.

"We wouldn't?"

"No. I'd still think all men are players. And you, being a man—"

He sends his hands up under my shirt and spreads his fingers around my ribs, then his thumbs rub along the underside of my breasts.

"Yes?" he asks.

I take his mouth and his hands rise up and he circles my nipples.

"A tallish, short-haired, hazel-eyed man," I say.

"And you being a medium-height..."

"Long-haired, blue-eyed woman."

"Exactly." He presses his mouth to my neck and kisses the underside of my jaw.

"I wouldn't like you. And you would..."

"Ask you to dinner," he says. He lifts his hips and his length hits me right...there. "Because, the minute I saw you, I'd realize that you were special and that I'd never felt this way about anyone before and—"

"I'd say no. Because I'd think you were a player and just using pick-up lines."

He cocks his hips again and I gasp. My clit throbs and each time he hits it a pulse of warmth rushes through me. I grab his shoulders and move against him.

"Then, when you said no, I'd try again," he says in a low, urgent voice. "I'd bring you flowers and ask you to come to New York City. I'd take you on my favorite walks in Central Park, you'd climb the boulders, then, we'd get coffee and cookies at this old Hungarian bakery I grew up by, and that night I'd take you home and make you pasta. We'd go to the roof deck, eat spaghetti, drink wine, and watch the sun set over the river."

I reach down and feel the thick ridge of him. His length jerks up when I touch him. I carefully undo his button and then unzip his fly. I take him in my hand. He's hot and smooth and I run my hand over him. He lets out a harsh exhale.

"I'd say no," I tell him. "I'd think you were pulling out all the player stops, tempting me with sunsets and wine and homemade dinners. I'd tell you to get lost."

He arches under me when I stroke my hand down his length. I revel at the feel of him in my hand. The softness, the heat. There's the smallest bit of moisture at the tip of him. I lean down and kiss him there, taste the salt of him.

His hands stop stroking me and then he carefully moves them down. He traces my stomach, the flare of my hips, and then he circles round and pushes my pants and panties down until he finds my clit.

He circles his finger over me and I cry out.

"Then, I'd try again. I'd ask you to go with me to New Zealand, to climb in Fiordland National Park. Or if that was too far, I'd take you to Italy to climb the Dolomites. We'd stay at a villa with a patio and an outdoor oven, and we'd drink Italian wine, and eat olives and fresh bread and—"

I kiss him and I can taste the Italian sun, olive groves, focaccia bread and red wine. His finger circles over my clit and then he sends a finger inside me. I cry out into his mouth and he pushes in deeper. I clench around him and I want more. I need more of him.

I grasp his length harder and stroke down, matching his rhythm.

"I'd say no," I tell him. Then I cry out as he puts another finger into me. "Tell you to leave me be. But I'd be intrigued, because players usually give up and find easier targets."

"But I'm not a player."

"No. And I also like tallish, short-haired, hazel-eyed men."

I can barely think anymore, I can only feel. His fingers inside me, his hand stroking my clit, his mouth, sucking my neck, kissing my jaw, his body warm and solid beneath me. The hot, hard, softness of him in my hand and the pressure I feel growing at his base. He throbs in my hand and I clench in response. I'm warm, I'm safe, and even though it's dark I feel like between us we have all the light in the world.

"I'd try again," he says, and his voice is rough and strained. "I'd keep trying. Because the more I saw you the more I'd know, you and I..." He stops as I clasp him tighter. Pump him up and down. He growls and I stroke him harder.

"Veronica," he says. "I can't—"

"We can." I kiss him.

He growls and something unleashes in him. He pulls me to him, sends his hands faster, harder. His mouth moves over me. Each sensation becomes a bright, throbbing light. His kiss, a spark. His hands inside me, a fire. And the growing, aching need...I shout out, ride the exquisite brightness...it's as bright as a star. I feel the heat of his cum. I clench around his hands in response, and I ride the shooting stars of my orgasm. Until finally, finally, I fall back to him and settle into the darkness.

I feel boneless and liquid. I stay on top of him, happier and more content than I have been in...ever.

And how strange is that? Considering we're staring death in the face.

Sam wraps his arms around me and runs a small circle over my back. I wonder why fate didn't pair me with Sam. If it had, I never would've run.

He feels like he should be mine.

"What would you do next?" I whisper. "After I said no again. After I told you to get lost and never come back?"

His hand pauses. "I guess I'd ask you to go on a walk."

"A walk?"

"If I couldn't entice you with dinners, or city lights, or

romantic trips, I'd ask if you'd like to go on a walk. You could be you, and I could be me, and we could walk together."

"Just walk?"

"That's right. I'd walk next to you and you'd walk next to me."

"And we could walk anywhere?"

"Wherever we liked."

"But we'd do it together?"

"That's right."

I rest my head against his chest and listen to his heart. "That sounds nice," I say.

I drift to sleep, lulled by his heartbeat and the soft rocking motion of his breath.

8

SAM

I WAKE Veronica after a few hours of sleep. We've been in the cave for thirty hours. A day and a night have passed since we were trapped. After last night, I want to get out of here more than anything. Before I met Veronica I was drifting. I was finally starting to head in the right direction, coming to Romeo, but I was still drifting. Now, everything is clear. I'm going to start my tech think tank, I'm going to move to Romeo, and I'm going to spend my life being worthy of her. That starts with getting us out of this cave.

My stomach gives a long growl and I try to push aside the fact that I haven't eaten since dinner at Evie's place. Unfortunately, I had coffee for breakfast on my way up from New York City and didn't eat before my hike.

"We should have some water," says Veronica.

We drink from the stalactite we found last night. Veronica and I take turns catching the slowly falling water droplets. My mouth is dry and the thirst hurts so much that it's painful to wait. It takes thirty minutes for us to swallow enough to quench our thirst. My stomach rumbles.

"How long can a person go without food?" I ask. Veronica knows more survival statistics than anyone I've ever met.

She's quiet for a moment, then, "It depends. Usually, anywhere from eight to twenty-one days. You have to account for hydration levels, exertion, the environment, the person's physical health and body composition."

"Are we on the lower end or the higher end of that range?" I ask. I hold my breath and wait for her answer.

She reaches over and threads her fingers through mine. I let out my breath.

"Roughly?" she asks. She playfully knocks her shoulder against mine. "Are you looking for an equation?"

I smile. "You could say that."

"Okay. Well, you can multiply my stubbornness by your determination and kick it to the power of twelve. So, I'd say we have all the time we need to find our way out of here."

"Roughly," I say.

She clasps my arm and squeezes. "Not roughly. My equation is exact."

Her stomach growls and we both ignore the sound. I do a separate calculation in my head. It's cold, we're using a lot of energy, and we aren't well hydrated. I'd say we may have more than a week, but not by much. And who knows how long we'll be able to keep moving once the effects of starvation and worsening dehydration set in. The clock is ticking.

"We should go," she says in a quiet voice. Maybe she was having the same thoughts.

I light my watch and we walk through the small room to the tight passageway.

"We'll have to crawl again," I say. We make sure the cairn and arrow are set up before moving on. We've been meticulous about marking our progress. Yesterday we hit so many dead ends and forks that we would've been wandering in circles without them. As it is, we're wandering, but not in circles. I'll mark up this entire cave with arrows and cairns if I have to. But we're going to find our way out of here.

I crawl through the tight confines of passage and keep my watch lit. I hear Veronica curse.

"You alright?"

"Okay. Just cut my hand on a sharp rock."

"Do you need to stop?"

"No. It's just a scratch."

I nod, she's tough. I keep moving forward, careful to push aside loose rocks that could hurt her hands. The skin on my shins and knees burns, and the cuts that sealed after yesterday's crawl open up again.

I hear Veronica sniff, it sounds like tears, and I remember yesterday in the tight, coffin-like crawl that she needed a story. "Do you remember the Greek myth about the minotaur?" I ask.

"The half-man, half-bull in the maze?"

"That's right. It was a labyrinth, an impossible maze built by Daedalus and his son Icarus."

"The Icarus who flew too close to the sun?"

"That's him. The minotaur was the son of the queen of Crete and her lover, a bull. The Queen's husband, King Minos, caged the minotaur in the labyrinth and demanded the Athenians send seven maidens and seven youths every nine years for the minotaur to eat."

"Gross. Please tell me we aren't crawling toward a man-eating minotaur."

I chuckle and squeeze up and over a stone mound. The tunnel is widening a bit and there's more room to crawl.

"Theseus, the King of Athens' son, volunteers to go for the third tribute and swears he'll kill the bull."

"Brave."

They always were. Brave and foolish. "When he got there, the King of Crete's daughter, Ariadne, fell in love with him. She begged Daedalus to tell her how to defeat the maze. Before Theseus went in she gave him a ball of string. He let it out behind him, found the minotaur, killed it in battle, and then followed the string back out."

"If only I had my pack. I had a rope in there."

I grin. "I think we're in a modern day labyrinth and the cairns and arrows are our string. We'll find our way out, just like Theseus."

"Mmm. So, did Ariadne and Theseus live happily ever after? Isn't that how these stories go?"

I'm silent for a moment. Then, "Well. They sailed off together. But then, Theseus abandoned Ariadne on a deserted island and married her sister instead."

There's a gasp and then Veronica starts to laugh. "You've got to be kidding me. There were jerk players in Ancient Greece? Don't tell me I'm Ariadne and you're Theseus. I'll leave your butt in this freaking maze."

I start to laugh. I feel her move behind me, she swats at my thigh. I reach behind me and catch her hand, then I maneuver around so that I'm on my back and she's on top of me. The tunnel is three foot high, plenty of room.

I hold her in place and she squirms against me.

"I'm not Theseus," I say. "You're not Ariadne."

"Obviously," she says and she stops squirming.

"But we are using Daedalus's string, it's our cairns, and we will get out of here."

"Obviously," she says again. "Besides, I don't have a sister."

"And if I were Theseus, I'd never leave you," I say. "If you led me out of a labyrinth and saved my life, I'd have to be insane to let you go."

"Insane, or a player," she says.

My mouth twists. What will she say when she finally sees my face? Learns my past?

"What if I was?"

"But you aren't."

My heart thuds painfully against her. I squeeze her to me. "No. But other people said I was. Most everyone believed I was."

"Who didn't?"

"My family."

"Well. There you go."

Her hair falls over my cheek and I rub it between my fingers.

"What happened to Ariadne?" she asks.

I think back to the story. "She married a god. Dionysus."

"The god of wine and partying?"

"That's right."

She snorts and lays her head on my chest. "What was the appeal? He sounds like a bigger player than Theseus."

"I don't know. I imagine he loved her."

She's quiet for a moment and then she reaches up and runs her hand over my chin. "So, I guess it all worked out after all."

She presses a kiss to my mouth and I savor the taste of her and the feel of her. She feels so good that there's a sound in my ears, almost like singing. Except...

She pulls away. "Do you hear that?"

"What is it?"

"I don't know."

She scrambles back and I right myself. We start back down the passage, making our way over the rocky terrain. As we go, the sound becomes louder. It's an echoing of voices, whispering and then gurgled laughter. It sounds almost, but not quite, human. The hair stands up on the back of my neck. I don't know what's ahead of us. Maybe it is a minotaur, or some other animal that lives in the depths of this dark cave.

Veronica is quiet behind me. Neither of us speaks as the noise grows louder. I let my watch light fade. The air moves faster and I feel mist hit my face. The voices are gone, instead we're surrounded by a rushing noise. I reach overhead and realize that I can stand. I step up and stretch. I light my watch and hold out my arm. Behind me, Veronica gasps.

The blue light catches and reflects off sprays of water floating through the air. A fine mist, like a cloud swirls around. Veronica steps forward and takes my hand.

"It's a waterfall," she says. "An underground waterfall."

We step forward to the edge of a small, swiftly moving stream. It's a foot wide, and the water cuts deep into the white limestone. I hold the light over the stream and follow it up the slope. Ten feet up, there's a curtain of water running over the milky flowing stone of the cave wall.

"How high is it?" Veronica asks.

I hold my watch as high as I can. The waterfall glows in the light as far as I can see. The chattering, gurgling voices come from the water running over the stone and falling through cracks and holes and rock formations.

"I don't know," I say. "At least twenty feet." The light of the watch ends far below the top of the waterfall.

I put my hand into the waterfall. It runs through my fingers and feels like cold silk, the current pushes my hand lower.

"Do you think anyone has ever seen this before?" Veronica asks.

She reaches into the falls and lets the water run over her hands. I tangle my fingers with hers. We listen to the cacophony of the waterfall, the song of the mist, and the tinkling music of the droplets falling from the stalactites.

"I don't know," I say. "I hope so."

That would mean someone has been here before, and left again. But also that someone else has experienced this wonder. I hold up my arm again and try to reflect the light off the water's surface. The waterfall empties into a stream that leads to a small shallow pool. It glows a clear azure, as pure blue as glacier ice. Stalactites and stalagmites crowd the room twisting up and around and glowing with crystalline light.

"It's like another world," Veronica says. There's awe in her voice.

I try to see her face. Her expression. I catch the brightness of her hair, it's light brown or blonde. Her skin is pale. Beyond that, the light's too dim. But in this room, with the mist floating around us and the chorus of voices from the waterfall, I wonder if I've dreamed her.

No, she's real. And I know one thing for certain.

"You're beautiful," I say.

She laughs and flicks a spray of water at me. "You can't even see me. You have no idea what I look like."

"I know exactly what you look like," I say.

She grabs my hand and we move through the cavern. I shine my light at the ground so we don't trip or fall into an unexpected gap.

"Alright, what do I look like?"

"You're about five foot seven. Slight but athletic."

"That's easy, what else?"

"You're strong. It's in the way you stand. Straight and assured, with your chin tilted up like you're ready to take on the world."

I touch the line of her jaw, and her chin is tilted up just like I described.

"How did you—"

I continue.

"You have a soft mouth, a kind mouth, but you bite your

bottom lip a lot because you're always thinking, trying to work out what to do next."

I rub my finger over her lip and feel the contradiction of softness and strength. She pulls in a breath and her lips soften under my touch.

"When you walk in a room, people notice you and respect you, but they like you too, because you have a kind smile and warm eyes. Your skin is sun-kissed, because you love the outdoors, and you take the time to appreciate nature. And your fingers are calloused because you climb, but also because you work hard at everything you do, whether it's surviving in a cave or building a business from the ground up. You're strong, soft, sweet and determined. Like I said, beautiful."

She's silent for so long that I wonder if I've said too much. Gone too far, too fast. But then she relaxes against me.

"Thank you," she says.

"You're welcome."

"I guess you do see me."

I press her into my side and breathe in the scent of her. I close my eyes and imagine us together, outside of this cave.

"Do you think..." She pauses.

"What?"

"When we get out of here, that this will fade? That we only feel this way because of the circumstances? Supposedly, I have a soul mate. I don't want him. Ever. But...you know, people get close in extreme circumstances, and then when it's over they don't ever see each other again. And...Erma, the soul mate seer, she's never wrong. If we keep this up, keep getting close, it's likely we're setting ourselves up for heartbreak."

My chest clenches and her words send a jolt of fear through me.

"I don't agree," I say. "It won't fade. What I feel for you..."

"Yes?"

"It won't fade."

She takes my hand. "I know."

"Tell me about this psychic again. And your soul mate."

We pick our way through the cavern, wordlessly agreeing to find a path forward. We're going to make it out of here, and Veronica's fears won't come true. I feel certain, just as I felt at age nine when I knew I was meant to work with computers the rest of my life, that we're meant to be together. We fit.

"He's like my dad," she says after a moment of silence.

"He's not the right guy then."

I feel her nod. "He's wealthy and he throws his money around. Uses it to lure women in. Instead of using a cute daughter, he uses wealth to buy women."

I have an uncomfortable itch between my shoulder blades. This schmuck sounds similar to the man I was trying to become.

"No redeeming qualities?"

"None. Not a single one. He repulses me. There's nothing he could say or do to make me want to be with him."

I roll my shoulders and try to alleviate the feeling between my shoulder blades. I'm not the man she's talking about. Thank God. If I were, I'd deserve her rejection.

"What if he reforms? Falls in love with you and becomes a better man?"

She snorts. "That sort of thing doesn't happen in real life. He's either a player, a wanna-be player, or a good guy. And he's not a good guy."

"But your friend's aunt says you're supposed to be together?" I'm still having a hard time wrapping my head around this psychic-predicting-soul-mates situation. "And she's never wrong?"

I feel Veronica shrug. "Doesn't matter if she's right or not. I decide my own fate." She pokes me in the side, "I'll never be with him, I promise."

I let out a long breath. "Good. If you do, I'll remind you of your promise and make sure you keep it."

"So sure of your appeal?"

I smile. "No. But we're in a cave and you don't have much choice. It's either me or the rocks."

We've circled the cavern and found the only passage out. We stand before it and take it all in. From what I can see, it's two sheer rock walls, about two feet apart leading across a chasm. I drop a rock and count the seconds.

"Forty-four feet," I say.

We have to wedge ourselves between the walls, suspend ourselves over the chasm, and climb across.

There's no other exit, except the passage we came out of.

"Forward?" asks Veronica.

I think about what going forward means. Maybe we die. Or we find a way out, Veronica sees who I am...maybe leaves me. Or she finds her soul mate and decides on him after all. Or we stay together, spend the rest of our lives together. My heart beats against my ribs. That. That's what I want.

She's the one.

"Forward," I say.

9

VERONICA

I TAKE A DEEP BREATH. I've done climbing techniques similar to this before. It's a moderate-width opening. I feel the walls on either side of the crevice. It's dry, rough-textured and solid.

"I'm going first," I say.

I feel Sam tense. He's going to argue with me. I've noticed he likes to be in front in case there's any danger. If someone's going to fall or have rock collapse on them, he'd rather it be him. I touch his arm and he stills.

"I've got this. We don't know how narrow it'll get or if it's stable. I'm smaller. I can have us turn around if it gets too dangerous."

"Makes sense," he says, but I can tell he doesn't like it.

"Have you climbed before?" I ask.

"Indoor walls," he says. "I've been doing them a couple years now."

I smile and squeeze his arm. "Look at you. When we get out of here, I'm going to take you to my favorite climbs. The Gunks, the Red River Gorge. You'll love climbing outdoors. We could go up to the Adirondacks, take a tent, sleeping bags..." I stop.

"On second thought, when we get out of here, I'd like food, a shower, and a bed. Climbing can wait."

"I'd love to," he says.

"The climbing or the shower and the bed?"

"Any of it."

I reach up and touch his face. I trace his mouth and feel his smile.

Then I pull away and concentrate on the climb, getting us across the pit alive and hopefully to the way out. "We're going to use counterforce to keep us wedged between the walls. We'll start with our back flat against the wall on the right side. Put your right hand on the opposite wall, as high as your chest, and put your left hand behind you, lower than your back, and then press against it, out and down. Hard."

"Got it," he says.

"Your legs, it depends on your size. I'm probably going to have my right leg bent with my toes pressed into the wall and my left leg bent and my foot flat against the right wall."

"Makes sense. The counterforce is between your hands and legs on the opposite walls?"

"Exactly. You might have to use your hands and knees, you're at least half a foot taller than me. But keep your arms on opposite walls. As long as we do that and keep pressing, we should be okay."

"Alright."

Before I can move into the crack, he pulls me to him and sets a hard kiss on my mouth. His hands curl around my arms and his grip bites into me. The kiss is fierce and quick.

"For luck," he says.

I step to the ledge and work myself into the crack. I do just as I planned and within seconds I'm suspended over a forty-four-foot drop. My back presses to the cold hard rock and my hands and feet shove against it and down. I inch myself forward, scraping along the rough rock. It's solid, I don't feel any weak spots in the limestone.

"Your turn," I say. I've moved in enough that he can climb up behind me.

I shimmy forward and listen as the rocks scrape against his shoes and shorts.

"I'm in," he says. His voice is strained.

I concentrate on keeping the counterpressure between my limbs. There's no rope to catch me if I fall. I shift my hand then my foot, my next hand, then my opposite foot. The cut on my palm from the crawl starts to burn. I feel wetness and realize that it's bleeding again. The blood makes the rock slick and my hand shakes against the wall.

"You alright?" Sam asks.

"Good. I'm good," I say. This maneuver is strenuous even when you're rested. My legs start to shake. I press my opposite leg harder, then quickly drop my hand to my shirt and wipe the blood off. I hiss at the sting.

We've gone at least ten feet. I can't see in front of me to know whether we're close to the end of the crack. I can't see anything at all. Sam's watch light has gone off and he's not in a position to turn it back on.

I shift my back and inch my way forward. My right foot jams forward, moving faster than I intended. Rock from the wall comes loose and clatters to the bottom of the pit. My limbs shake and sweat trickles down into my eyes.

I wipe my hand again. The blood oozing out makes it hard to keep my hand flat against the rock.

Sam swears. I hear rocks smash against the bottom of the pit.

"Okay?"

"Hit a loose spot."

My heart thuds in my chest, ramming against my ribs. My

legs and arms burn with the exertion. I concentrate on moving forward. Shift, slide, press, move. Shift, slide, press, move. Inch forward. Don't fall. Wipe the blood. Shift, slide, press, move.

Sam's moving faster than me. He's caught up to me. I feel his hand brush against mine as he slides forward. His breath is harsh and loud.

"Hey you," I say. My limbs shake.

"Fancy meeting you here," he says.

I inch forward. Press, slide. Wipe the blood.

"Whatcha doing?" he asks in a light, playful voice. He's trying to cut the tension.

"Oh," I grunt, "just hanging out."

"Come here often?" he asks.

"Only on Tuesdays," I say.

"And Sundays. It's Sunday."

"Fancy that."

He laughs. "Just hanging out. Tuesdays and Sundays."

I smile.

Suddenly, my bloody hand slips, to compensate I jam my foot harder against the wall. But the rock's loose. It crumbles away and my back slides down the wall. I start to fall.

"Sam!"

The rock tears at my back. My hand claws at the rock. My feet slip. My stomach rises up and this is it, I'm...

"Got you."

Sam catches me. He grabs my arm. Levers himself against the wall and lifts me back up into the crack. I wedge my feet into the wall and wipe my bloody hand on my shirt. Press my shaking hands into the walls. I'm cold and sweating. I think I'm going to be sick. The sound of my pounding heart fills my ears. It's dark. It's too dark. I'm shaking. My limbs can't hold on.

"We've got to quit meeting like this," Sam says. He presses his thigh against mine. "You falling. Me catching."

I let out a half-laugh, half-sob.

Then, I close my eyes and re-center myself. Better. I blow out a long, steadying breath. "One of these days, I'm going to catch you," I say.

"Looking forward to it."

He brushes his fingers over mine.

A second later, "You okay?" he asks.

I swallow down the rising fear and try not to think about the open crevice beneath me.

"I'm great. Like I said, just hanging out."

"Good."

I start moving again. I wipe my hand every few seconds to keep it dry. My arms and legs burn and ache. They're screaming at me to straighten out, but we're not to the end yet.

Sam hits his watch display and I breathe a sigh of relief.

"We made it."

I scoot another foot then drop down. My legs shake and cramp and I drop to the cold rock. Sam lands next to me. He sits down and pulls me into his lap.

We don't say anything. We just sit there, breathing hard, relishing the hard ground beneath us. His heart pounds against my back. His arms shake and he pulls me harder against his chest. I rub my face against him and wait for his heartbeat to slow.

Finally, my arms and legs stop aching, my hand stops bleeding, and my heart stops racing.

His fingers tangle in my hair and drift over my back. The familiar movement of his hands on me brings me back to a calm place. His touch is the only light I have. There's the soft, reassuring touch of his fingers to my lips, like the golden light of dawn. When his hands circle and drift over my back, it's the gentle, breezy light of mid-afternoon. The hard grip of his hand in mine is the bright clear light of a sunny afternoon. The touch of his lips pressing against mine is the dusky, purple light of evening. And when he touches me with want and need, it's the light of a thousand sunsets.

He brushes a kiss to my forehead, at the corner of my eye. I see the light of stars shining in the darkness.

"You saved me," I say.

He presses a kiss over each of my eyelids.

"I told you I'd get you out of here. I can't do that if you're at the bottom of a pit."

"Well, that's true."

"Besides, you promised me a shower and a bed. I'd do just about anything for a shower."

I wrinkle my nose. He's right. It smells really bad. Like musty ammonia, but worse.

"Do you smell that?" I ask.

"It's coming off that draft," he says.

I stand and sniff the air. Sure enough, there's a slight breeze coming from the wall behind us. There's something tickling my mind, a memory, or a thought. Then there's a noise. A scratch, then a squeak.

"Bats," I say. "Bats!"

I grab Sam and start jumping up and down. I hug him to me.

"What? What is it?"

"It's bats. That smell is bat pee. There's gotta be a whole colony."

He stops, and then what I said sinks in because he pulls me to him and lets out a whoop.

"Bats," he says. "Thank the lord for bats."

Then he kisses me and I jump into his arms. I smile against his mouth.

"We're getting out of here."

The bats are going to show us the way out.

10

SAM

FIFTY-TWO HOURS later we're still in the cave. We followed the stench of ammonia through tight cracks, up natural stairs, through tunnels and more dead ends than I can count. But we haven't found the bat colony or a way out.

I can hear them off and on, squeaking and scratching, but I can't pinpoint where the sound is coming from. The echo could be traveling from far away, through a small crack in the stone for all I know, or through a twisted labyrinth of turns that we haven't managed to crack.

I don't know what to do. We've been in this cave for more than four days. Veronica hasn't complained, but I know she's getting weaker. Sometimes she stumbles over rocks or grabs at the walls to support herself. She was sure-footed when we started this trek, and the fact that she's not anymore tells me that time's running out. We stop more often for drink breaks and huddle together for rest more often. Time is pressing down on us, but there's no way I'm giving up. If Veronica passes out from hunger and I can't stand anymore, I will crawl and drag her out on my back. I'm not giving up.

We stand in front of a small tunnel. Veronica sniffs, the smell of bats is strong and there's a slight draft.

"This is the way," she says. "I swear I hear them through there." Her voice is less confident though; we thought we'd found the path to the colony dozens of times over the past two days.

I kneel down and set up a cairn and an arrow. If she's right, we'll not see it again. There's a squeak and I tilt my head.

"Did you hear that?" she whispers.

We remain quiet and unmoving, but the noise doesn't come again.

I stand and measure the tunnel with my hands. The rock is hard and unyielding, cold and quiet. I've learned a lot about this cave over the past few days. The caverns, the tunnels, the streams and pools, the formations and stalagmites, all of them have a different personality, a feeling they emanate. Some spaces are quiet, like they are watching or listening as we pass through. Others, like the waterfall cavern, are full of energy and mischief, and the water sounds like it's laughing. There are spaces that feel ominous, others that are peaceful and silent, like the feeling that comes just before falling asleep. This tunnel has a unique feeling. I can't describe it, except that it gives me a strange feeling in the pit of my stomach. I felt the same way once as a ten-year-old kid. I walked through Central Park alone one night and when I saw a group of teens on the path ahead I had this same feeling. Instead of turning around and going another way I went forward. I was beaten and robbed.

I feel the rock of the tunnel and span the circumference of the entry.

"It's going to be tight." The narrowest yet.

The squeaking noise comes again. Then, there's the flapping of wings and a disturbance of air next to my cheek.

"Did you feel that?"

"It went into the tunnel?" she asks, her voice is filled with hope.

"It did. It flew right past me."

That settles it. Strange feeling in the pit of my stomach or not, this is the way out.

Veronica moves next to me. I light my watch and she peers into the dark space. It looks like a coffin, tight and smooth and dark. "Should I go first?" she asks. Her voice shakes. There's no question about it, she hates the feeling of being closed in.

"Good idea," I say.

She bends over and starts to climb in. "Wait," I say. I unstrap the watch from my wrist. "Take this."

I put the metal watchband around her wrist, it's too big by a few links, but I click it into place then push it up her forearm. I settle my hand on her arm, press it over the watch. She reaches out and presses her hands against my chest. "The button on the side lights it," I say. "In case you need the light closer to you." Having the glow nearby should help her make it through.

"Thank you," she whispers.

"Of course. You can give it back when we make it to the end of this tunnel. We'll be at the exit and you won't need it anymore."

"Exactly," she says. Then she turns and starts into the tunnel.

It's the same as every other tight space we've shimmied through, except not. It's tighter, my shoulders barely fit through some of the gaps, and the feeling...it's unsettling.

"Tell me again," says Veronica, "about your dreams for the future. Your business and your travels and your house in the country."

Her voice is muffled in the close confines, but I can hear her mounting anxiety. It's hard when we're in these coffin-like spaces not to think about getting stuck and never making it out. Talking helps.

Over the past few days, Veronica and I have shared our dreams. Mine are new. I'm finally shedding the past and letting myself have new dreams. I've told her my plans to renovate a house in the country, one near the White Pine Trail, and to make it a home. I've shared all the places I want to travel. We've brainstormed ideas for building my new business. She's told me about her greeting card company and I've helped her create a plan for growing her staff and going international. She's shared how she's going to be a godmother and how she'll spoil the baby and love her so much. I think about how much love Veronica has to give, how strong and brave and kind she is. I'm going to get us out of here.

"In my house," I begin, "I've thought of a new room."

"Yeah?"

"A climbing gym. It'll be three stories tall, full of complex holds and practice areas for difficult climbing techniques."

"Sounds nice," she says.

"It's for this woman I know. I really like her, and I'm hoping she'll want to live with me." I stop crawling and listen for her response. My chest tightens as I wait for her answer.

She doesn't speak for a bit, then, "What else will be at your house?" There's a smile in her voice.

I let out an exhale.

"She likes coffee. So in the kitchen I'm going to have an industrial setup. An espresso maker and a steamer, and I'll only buy the best coffee beans."

She makes a noise that I take as approval.

"She also doesn't like to be cold, so I'll put in fireplaces. One in the living room, another in the kitchen, one in the bedroom. And I'll have a hot tub and a sauna."

"Sounds expensive," she says.

"Does it?" I ask.

"This girl doesn't need you to go into debt for her. She'd be happy with a hot bath and some wool socks, maybe a blanket and a cuddle on a couch."

I smile. "So, do you think she'll want to move in with me?"

"What else will be in your house?" she asks.

"I was thinking a bed, a shower, a kitchen stocked with food."

"Now you're talking."

"And me. The house would come with me."

"Then I think she'd be crazy to refuse."

I send up thanks to heaven.

Then, "There's an incline. It's tight here," she says. I hear her boots scrape against the rock.

I move in after her, send my arms up and grab a rocky protrusion. I pull my arms through. The walls scrape my arms as I lift myself. Then, I stop. My heart starts to beat hard. I try to pull up, can't…I try to push down…can't.

Veronica moves forward. The light of the watch grows dimmer.

"Veronica," I say. My voice is a sharp gasp. I've wedged my ribs between the walls of the inclining tunnel and I can't pull myself out. "Veronica," I say more sharply.

She stops. "Are you okay?"

"I'm stuck," I say.

My ribs start to ache and it's hard to breathe. She crawls back to me. The walls are too close for her to turn around, so she lays down on the ground and flips onto her back. She scoots on her back until she's next to my extended arms.

"I pull you through," she says.

My throat tightens. "No," I say. "Too tight." I'm running out of air. I jammed myself in and my lungs are compressed. I'm taking short, painful breaths.

"Sam?" Her voice is small and scared.

I lever my hands on the ground and try to shove myself back. I can't. I'm stuck.

"Push me back," I say. "Kick..." with your feet, I want to say, but it's taking too much air to speak.

She puts her boots on my shoulders and presses as hard as she can. I grunt at the pressure. The sides of the rock squeeze down on my ribs and her boots dig into my shoulders. There's a sharp painful stabbing in my chest.

"Sam? Can you...can you just pull through?"

"Can't..." Red and blue sparks light in front of my eyes. The pain in my chest grows and my lungs ache every time I pull in a short breath.

Suddenly, I'm dizzy. My head feels heavy. The darkness is different now, like it's coming from me rather than the cave. The rocks are crushing my ribs, crushing my lungs.

My head drops to my chest. I try to pull it back up but I can't. My hands claw at the earth, I push back...pull...nothing. I try to pull in another breath, but there's no air.

"Sam?" I hear panic in Veronica's voice. Fear.

But I can't answer. Can't reassure her. I don't have enough air.

This isn't the end, it can't be.

My thoughts jumble. Spin together. I see Veronica, the picture that I have of her in my mind, she floats in front of me. I see us walking toward our house. We're holding hands. I turn and kiss her, carry her over the threshold.

I desperately try to pull in air, to fill my compressed lungs. My head swims, falls forward. My forehead smacks against the rock. I want to tell her...need to tell her something. I thought we were going to get out of here. I'd hoped...

She still can. She can follow this out.

With my last bit of air I bite out, "Go."

Then I slip back into the vision of us walking into our home, but when I open the door, step inside, it's dark and she's gone.

11

"Sam?" I cry out. He doesn't answer. There's nothing but the forbidding silence of the tunnel. "Sam!" Nothing. My heart jerks in my chest. "Answer me." He doesn't. I hit the watch light and the dim glow outlines his figure. My heart lurches and bile rises in my throat.

"Sam, move. Push."

He doesn't. He can't.

His head lies at an awkward angle on the ground, his arms sprawl in front of him, his hands are open and still. He doesn't move.

"Sam," I shout. "Please."

Nothing. My stomach turns and I fight down rising nausea. He's stuck. He's...suffocating?

"No. Sam. No." I jerk myself across the ground, inching closer to him.

"Talk to me. Sam." My hands reach his face. His skin is cool, I can't feel his breath, he's as still as the walls of this godforsaken cave. My hands shake, my heart thunders, I can't hear, I can't think.

"Sam? Move. Pull yourself through." From somewhere outside me, I realize that I'm not thinking clearly. That he's unconscious and can't hear me. "Please. Please!"

My legs brush against his arms and they flop to the side, completely without the life or strength that I'm used to. He's...he's dead? Dying? The light of the watch goes out and we plunge into darkness. I can't see him, I can't hear him, he's left me. He's gone.

"Sam! Wake up. If you leave me in this cave I will kill you. Do you hear me? I will come after you, follow you in death and I will kill you. Do you hear me?"

He doesn't answer. There's no sound, and he doesn't even twitch. Thirty seconds has passed since he told me to *go*. A sob escapes me and I shove it back down. I won't cry. He's not gone. I can fix this. How dare he tell me to go? We're together. We're in this together and I'm never going to leave him.

I love him.

I love him.

I realize that love hasn't made me weak, it's made me strong. I couldn't have made it this far without him. He's given me support and kindness, courage and friendship...I love him, I can't...

"Please don't leave me," I say. "I need you. I need you here with me. We're doing this together. We're getting out of here together. Please, Sam. Please."

Nothing. Just the stillness of the walls pressing the life from him.

"I'll move in with you and help you remodel your house," I promise him. "I'll go with you to Italy. We'll eat olives and drink wine. I'll come with you to New York and meet your family and have your mom's pasta. We'll walk together. Remember? You promised me we'd walk together. I want to meet you. I want to meet you outside of this cave. Please, Sam. Please."

I brace my feet against the walls. His ribs are jammed between the rock. He's stuck tight and doesn't even have enough room for breath. I have to get him out.

I wedge my feet against the edge of the walls, angle myself to give myself as much leverage as possible. Then I grasp him under his arms.

"Come on." I pull on him. He's at least one hundred and seventy-five pounds, tall and muscular. He's not budging.

"Come on," I cry. I push with my legs against the walls and yank as hard as I can. "Please, Sam. I love you. Please."

Then all the love I feel for him, the desperation of him leaving me, it fills me and I push against the stone and yank as hard as I can. Suddenly, I'm falling backwards, because Sam has inched forward and cleared the rocks.

I cry out then grab him again. The tunnel widens ahead, at least to three feet in height. I pull him forward and over me. Then, I roll onto him and press into him. I squeeze over him and run my hands across him, try to hear a breath, find his heartbeat.

I can't.

But then I feel the solid thud of his heart beneath my hand. Cold, stunned relief washes over me. Then his chest bows and he drags in a ragged gasping breath. His body tenses and he tries to sit up.

"I'm here," I say. I push him back down to the ground. "It's okay. You're okay. I'm here."

He pulls in raw, gasping breaths, his chest heaving. Then, "Veronica?"

"I'm here." My voice is thick with tears. "I'm here."

"I thought…" He draws in another breath.

"Don't ever do that again," I tell him.

His arms shake. Then he wraps them around me and

presses me tightly to him. I concentrate on the rise and fall of his chest and the thundering of his heart.

"Never again," I say. "Never again."

He moves his hands over me, across my shoulders and back, down my hips and across my thighs. The movement of his hands on me feels like the warmth of the sun on a summer day. He's here. He didn't leave me.

I thread my fingers through his hair and lift his mouth to mine. I press my lips over his and take his mouth and his breath and I thank heaven that he still has breath to give.

"You were crying," he says, surprised. I think he can taste the salt of tears on my mouth.

I press my forehead to his, rub my nose over his, and let my lips hover against his breath. He reaches up and presses his thumbs against my cheeks. He stiffens when he feels the wetness of my tears.

"Don't cry," he says.

Then he wipes his hands down my skin, drawing away the tears.

"Don't cry," he whispers again. "I'm here. I'm not leaving you."

He presses his lips to my cheeks and my eyelids, kissing away the fear. A small sob escapes me and he pulls me against his chest.

"We're almost out of here. It'll be alright."

He runs his hands soothingly over my back.

"I'm alright. It'll be alright," he says.

"It'll be alright," I repeat. But I don't know that I believe him. I don't know that we'll ever make it out of here, or that if we do, everything *will* be alright. We can't know what's going to happen. One minute, the person you love can be right next to you, then next minute they could be gone.

I settle into him. Safe in the cocoon of his arms, his breath rising and his heartbeat echoing mine. His hands lift up and tangle in my hair. Then his fingers drift down my face and his touch is gentle, soft, almost...reverent.

"Veronica?"

"Yes?"

He draws his fingers over my eyelids, my nose, my cheek, neck and collarbone. His touch sends shooting stars across my skin. I fall into the tinkling liquid warmth of his fingers running over me.

"I...I need you to know...I love you. More than anything in the world. If something happens again, I don't want to leave this world without you knowing how I feel. I love you, more than any person has the right to love another. Especially since I've never seen your face, or gotten coffee with you, or taken you out on a date, I've not done any of the things a man does to show a woman he loves her. And you've not seen me, you don't know what I look like, or who I am in the outside world, what I'm like. It's selfish of me to say this, but I have to tell you. I love you. And I'm not asking you to love me back, I only want you to know that I love you. So much. We may not make it out of here, but I can't be sorry about it, because being here means I got to meet you. And I'd rather die having these last four days with you than live another sixty years without."

His hands linger over me and I press myself into him.

"Is that alright?" he asks.

And I warm at the worry in his voice. He's afraid that I don't feel the same way. But how can he even think that? I bury my face against his neck and press a kiss into his pulse. His muscles tense, like he's waiting for me to deny him. But how could I?

"You think I haven't seen you? That I don't know what you're like in the outside world?" I ask.

His fingers still on me and I continue.

"We've been in here for four days. And four days cave time is like four years outside world time."

I brush my lips against his mouth.

"I see you," I say. "I know you."

I straddle his hips with my legs and lean over his face. I run my fingertips over his brow.

"You're smart and driven. You care about making the world a better place." I run my fingers over his eyebrows and then down his temples. "In the past, you trusted the wrong people and were hurt. Now, you don't trust as easily, and you're close to only a select few. But once you give your friendship, you'll do anything for them."

"That's right," he says.

I move my hands to his mouth and press them against the firm line of his lips. I run my fingers through the long stubble on his jaw and neck. His pulse picks up speed.

"You like family, and home, and quiet nights. You're generous and strong."

"Yes," he says.

I lean down and press a kiss to his mouth. He doesn't care about money or material things. In fact, it's likely that he makes less per year than I do. And he's not a player. He was faithful to his wife and then had a few rebound dates to get over her.

I pull my mouth from his. "You have plans for the future," I continue. "And you never give up."

I move my hands under his shirt and then run my fingers up the bare skin of his stomach and chest. I feel the hollow of his stomach, the flat muscles of his abdomen, his chest. I rest my hand over his heart.

"You are the best man I've ever known," I tell him. "And I trust you with my life."

I lift his shirt and then I pull it off him. He lets out a harsh breath.

"I know you," I say.

"I love you," he says.

I move to his shorts. Slowly pull them down his thighs. He kicks off his shoes. He's naked beneath me.

"I see you," I say.

"I love you," he says again, his voice is raw and an echo of all the emotion I feel inside.

I run my hands over his body. Explore him. The warmth of the skin near his heart. The strength of his shoulders. The curve of his elbow. His hands, confident and strong, but gentle whenever they touch me. The carved muscles of his abdomen, the jut of his hip bones. A small jagged scar on his thigh. A dusting of hair, a soft tickling against my skin. I trail my hands over his thigh and then brush against his length. He jerks beneath me and his hips lift. I close my hand around him. Sam hisses and his fingers dig into my thighs.

I grip him in my hand, feel the softness and the heat, the hardness of him. I lean down and kiss the tip of him. He pulses in my hand and I feel an aching need in response.

Then I let him go, lay on him and move up to his mouth. I press my lips to his and taste him. Feel him under me. The rightness of us.

"I love you," I whisper against him.

That's all it takes. He rolls me under him, shoves my shirt over my head. I kick off my boots and he yanks my pants down.

I let out a harsh breath when he spreads his body over mine. I barely notice the cold or the hard rock beneath me. My entire being, all my senses, are engulfed by him. His legs over mine, his hips pressing against mine, his arms wrapped around me. The beating of his heart against my chest. He runs the stubble of his cheek against my face and I shiver. Then he catches my lips and sends his tongue into my mouth. I suck on it and taste him. The salty, minerally limestone of the water we drink and the maleness that is purely Sam. He moves his hips and runs his length over me. He hisses when he feels how wet I am. The tip of him hits my entrance, but he stops and slides over my clit. I cry out and raise my hips to him. He brings his mouth over mine, and as he runs his length over my clit, he sends his tongue in and out of my mouth. I'm drugged by the rhythm he's making. I rise up to meet him and fall when he pulls away. He moves his hands over me, teases my breasts, circles my nipples. Everywhere he touches a spark lights, until I'm glowing, feeling so much fire that I'm surprised the tunnel isn't burning with the light we're making. He keeps running his length over me, spreading the heat through me. It builds, until the only thing I can concentrate on is the next time he's going to hit me...there. I roll my hips and I want...I want him inside me more than anything. I want to be joined with him, to become...his.

He reaches up, draws his hands up my arms, my wrists, then he threads his fingers through mine.

"Hold my hand," he says.

I clasp his hands and cry out when his length drives over my clit.

"Thank you," he whispers.

"You're welcome," I say.

Then he pauses at my entrance. I tilt my hips up, meet him there.

"I love you," he says.

Then, he thrusts his hips and I cry out as he fills me.

12

"I LOVE YOU," I say. And then I drive into Veronica. Everything disappears, the cave, the world, all of it vanishes except the two of us. The only thing that's real is our hands clasped together and her warmth and wetness wrapped around me.

I push into her, tilt her hips and push in as deep as I can. I hiss out a breath. She's tight and wet and I've never felt anything like her in my life. I want to stay this way forever, holding her to me, settled inside her, but I can't. I have to move.

I pull out and draw in a ragged breath at the sensation. She tightens around me and clenches as I pull out. Her hands clasp mine and she cries out. Then, I drive into her again. She clamps down on me and her warmth and tightness feel like heaven. I pull out and the world is dark, I drive in and there's light. Every time I leave her, there's only darkness and I feel like I might disappear, then when I join with her there's light and we're here. Together.

I grab her mouth. Taste her. I let go of one of her hands and reach down. Play with her swollen clit. Feel her pulse around me as I stroke her. She cries out my name.

"Yes," I say. "That's it."

I circle my fingers over her. Then I tilt up her hips and work myself in and out of her. I don't want this to end. If I could stay this way forever, I would. I never...I never want to live without her.

I cry out at the realization, plunge into her deeper, harder.

"Sam," she cries.

My name on her lips sends me over the edge. I feel the pressure, the thick building heat, and I drive harder, faster. I'm mindless for her. I only know that I need her, I want her, I love her.

Sparks and stars light behind my eyes.

Her walls clench around me, tighten down on me and I shout out. I'm so thick inside her that I can't do anything but drive in harder, deeper. Then the mounting pressure, the mindless need to bury myself so deep in her that I'll never leave, that I'll make her mine, it takes away all thought, I can only feel. She cries out and I feel her orgasm. I'm wedged so deep in her that I can't do anything but shout and ride her. I'm trapped, I'm trapped again, but this time, when I can't breathe and I can't move, I don't want to. I want to stay this way forever. With her. She grabs my back, pulls me closer and cries out.

"I love you," she sobs.

At her words, I can't hold on any longer. My cum rises up and explodes out of me in a wave of pleasure so intense that my mind goes blank. I can only feel her pulsing and pulling the cum from me as the world ignites. Light blinds me, a supernova, even though it's pitch black and there is no light, it's still there. It fills the world and I shout out.

All of it, everything is dragged out of me, pulled from me. And even when the waves stop, I still press into her, rock my hips against her, I don't want to leave. Don't want this to end.

I press a kiss to her mouth, rest my forehead against hers.

Eventually, my heartbeat slows, my breathing grows steady. I feel the cold, hard of the stone beneath my knees. The darkness of the tunnel. The chill of the air on my bare skin.

Veronica shifts beneath me and I reluctantly pull out of her.

"Was that okay?" I ask.

She sniffs, and I realize she's crying. My chest clenches.

"What's wrong?" Does she regret it? Maybe I shouldn't have...

"Nothing," she says. "It's just...I...I've never felt anything like that before."

I rub my fingers over her cheek, brush her tears away.

"Me either."

"Really?"

"Never."

"Thank you," she says. She reaches up and presses her hand against my jaw. "Thank you for being here."

She sounds almost sad. Like she thinks we aren't going to make it out of here. Like that was the last time she's ever going to experience anything like that. Determination fills me. This isn't the end.

I grab our clothes and we struggle back into them.

"We're getting out of here today," I say. My voice is filled with confidence. I know it. I don't know how I know it, but I do. We're getting out of here and then I'm going to make Veronica my wife. Because I can't imagine a future without her in it.

Veronica lights the watch and we crawl forward. The tunnel opens up and soon we're both walking upright. The smell of the bat colony grows heavier and I know we're on the right track.

I grab her hand and we move faster.

My heart is light. We're going to get out and I'm going to marry this courageous, loving woman. She won't care who I used to be, what mistakes I made, or what I did to get over my ex. She won't care about who the world thinks I am. She knows me, sees me. Loves me.

Suddenly, the tunnel ends and we drop down into a large cavern. From what I can see it's...

"Empty," says Veronica. "There's nothing here." Her voice is filled with shock and confusion. "I thought..."

We thought this was the way out.

It's dark, musty, full of bat guano and stink.

We walk around the cavern, feeling the edge of the walls, looking for a way out, but there's nothing. It's a dead end. We're still trapped.

I close my eyes and fight away the bitter sinking in my chest.

"It's okay," she says. "We can go back..."

She trails off. The knowledge sinks in and makes the air around us heavy. We can't go back. I'm too big for the tunnel. This time, I might not make it through alive. I was lucky to get through once. I'm stuck here. This is the end for me.

I grab her other hand and pull her to me.

"You can go," I say, resting my lips against her hair. I love her. I love her so much. I breathe in the scent of her, the warmth of her. I love her too much to keep her here to die with me. "You have to find another way out. Take the last fork that we didn't go down. Keep looking."

"No. Stop." She pushes at me. I pull her back and hold her close.

"Yes. Listen to me. This makes sense. Take the watch. You find a way out. You can get out, send rescuers back. I'll be fine here. There's plenty of water to drink. I'll rest up. I have what... another three to fifteen days before time runs out. You can find the way before then. This is what you've been waiting for, isn't it? The chance to rescue me?"

I kiss her hair.

She lets out a strangled laugh. "I don't want to rescue you, I want you to live."

A heaviness settles over me. Giving myself three days was generous, I know it, but I hope she doesn't. I've had a headache for more than a day now, my body is sore and sluggish, I'm becoming clumsy. I no longer feel hunger, just increasing weakness. I thought this was the exit, I'd thought we'd done it. But...no.

"I'll live," I tell her. "And so will you."

She shifts in my arms and lights the watch. I read the display, it's three in the morning of our fifth day in the caves.

Then, slowly and deliberately Veronica takes off the watch, unlatches the links and puts it back on my wrist. My heart wrenches as she does. She clasps the links and wraps her hands over the metal. Secures the watch in place. That's her answer. She's not taking the watch, she's not leaving me.

I swallow down my fear for her. The brave, stubborn woman.

"I'm not leaving you," she whispers. "I told you, we're in this together. I'm not leaving you."

She presses her hands to my checks and rests her lips to mine.

My shoulders fall. She won't try to save herself. She's so stubborn that she'll stay here with me to die rather than try to find a way out.

I shake my head. "I want you to go," I tell her. "I need you to keep looking."

"No. I'm not leaving you. I told you before, I don't want to die down here alone. I want to be with someone I know and trust. A friend."

She rests her head against my chest.

I know what she's envisioning. That she'll leave me here, and she won't find her way out, that she'll die alone at the bottom of a crevice or in a tunnel and I'll die alone in this stinking cavern. She's making a choice. I think it's the wrong one.

"Please don't," I say. "I need you to keep going. To get us out of here. I'll be with you"—I press my hand to her heart—"right here."

She sniffs and shakes her head then wraps her arms around me. I sink down to the ground and lean against the wall. She curls into me. Her hands wrap around my waist and she lays her head against my heart.

"We'll sleep for a bit," I whisper. I kiss her hair and rest my chin against her head. After she has some rest I'll convince her to leave me. To go, to keep fighting, to live.

I rub my hands over her back, the tension slowly fades from her and then her breathing steadies. She's asleep. I wrap my arms around her and try to memorize the feeling I have when I hold her. The warmth of her, the softness of her skin, the curve of her back and the flare of her hips. How even though it's dark, she shines bright for me.

For more than an hour I sit quietly, just holding her.

If she refuses to go, I'm going to have to take matters into my own hands. Years ago, when I was a kid, I went to the Race to the South Pole exhibit at the Natural History Museum. I remember Scott's party of British explorers were doomed. They were in an endless blizzard with no way out. They were going to die. One of the men had severe frostbite in his feet and he was slowing the party down. He knew he was harming the others' chances of survival, so he calmly told them he was going out for a walk and that he may be awhile. And then he left, walked into the white, and never returned. He sacrificed himself so the others could move faster. So he didn't ruin their slim chance of survival. This man walked into the darkness for his friends. As a child, I read the journals with horror and I didn't quite understand why he did it, but now I do. I understand. If Veronica refuses to leave, I'll have to do what that man did. Find a way to walk into the darkness, die so that she can survive. Make it to the light.

I shift her weight in my arms and pull her close.

"I love you," I whisper.

There's a sound above me. A squeaking and the humming of wings. I look up, then blink, because I think I see something. Which can't be right, because we're in a pitch black cave. But…I see movement and…

I shake Veronica. She wakes up with a start.

"What? What is it?" she asks sleepily.

"Look," I say.

I point toward the sound of the bats returning to roost. There must be hundreds of them. Thousands. They're flying into the cave from a hole in the ceiling. And we can *see* it. We can see it because it's five in the morning and there's the thin, gray light of dawn filtering down into the cavern.

It's dark, but I can see her. I can see Veronica.

We're going to live.

13

———————

VERONICA

THE MOUTH to the cave is twenty feet up a straight ledge. The sunrise filters in and looks like spidery gray webs as it lands on the rock and the returning bats. The bats fly past us, through the cavern and down the tunnel. I look up at the diving, swirling mass of them, and the rocky ledge, the light, and I start to cry. The tears fall from my eyes and I can't stop them. They pour out and my chest heaves as I let go of all the fear and desperation that we'd be trapped. That I would lose him.

Sam gathers me in his arms and holds me as the light continues to grow.

Finally, my tears stop and there's no more fear, just a peaceful feeling that everything's going to be alright and I'm exactly where I'm supposed to be. I look up, and for the first time get a look at the man I love.

The light's still dim, it's that early morning dark, but I can see him well enough.

My heart fills with love as my eyes follow the path of his face that my hands felt so many times.

He has a short thick beard. His hair has a cowlick and sticks up to one side. There's a mottled purple bruise on his left cheek his left eye is swollen half-way shut. Under his right eye is a cut covered in blood. He has deep, purple bags under his eyes and a worry line between his eyebrows. And he's filthy. His face is covered in dirt and dust. The rest of him doesn't look any better. His clothing is torn and dirty, his legs are scraped and raw.

I feel the beginning of a smile. Behind the dirt on his face, the bruise, the swollen black eye...I see him. I look into his eyes. They're exactly as I imagined. Warm, full of joy, awe. But strangely, I also see a hint of caution. As if he's concerned with what I'll think of him now that I can see his face.

I reach up and trace my hand down his jaw. "There you are," I say. "Tallish. Short hair. Hazel eyes. Exactly as I imagined."

He drops his head against my hand and lets out a long exhale.

"Just think, after we shower and eat, and the sun comes up I'll be able to see all of you. Meet you in the outside world," I say.

"It's a date," he whispers roughly.

And then he smiles at me and I catch my breath. I stare into his eyes and we grin like two fools who have just beaten the longest odds and won the world as our prize.

"I was right," he says.

"About what?"

"You're beautiful."

Right now, I can only imagine what I look like. Probably worse than he does. But he's not looking at my hair, or my body, or my clothes. He's looking into my eyes. My heart turns over. I'm his.

I look up at the ledge. It's an easy climb, there are plenty of handholds and footholds. Even exhausted and weak from hunger, we'll be able to climb out in minutes. I turn to Sam.

"Let's get out of here," I say.

I lead the way, working out the best route. I was right, in less than five minutes we're both standing next to a small rock outcropping, the cave mouth is hidden by the surrounding rocks. I grab Sam's hand and pull him close.

The soft, golden light of sunrise filters through the trees. Morning sounds fill the air, birds waking, chipmunks chattering. The crisp scent of pine needles and moss hits me. I pull in a deep, fortifying breath. I'm so grateful that I'll never, ever have to smell wet limestone and dank earth again.

I take a moment to take in the open air, the breeze tangling though my hair, the sun falling across my skin, the noises around me. The life.

"We did it," I say.

Sam squeezes my hand.

"Do you know where we are?" he asks.

I look around, try to see any landmarks I recognize. I face the direction of the sunrise. East. I'm not sure where we came out, whether we're miles from our original position or mere meters. The White Pine Trail is in a large swath of forest, but I know almost every inch of it.

"I don't," I say, "but if we head east, we're bound to come to civilization. The forest's eastern boundary butts against the freeway."

He lets out a relieved sigh. "Okay. Let's get hiking then."

I'm worried, we need to get food soon. I estimate the highway is anywhere from five to twenty miles away. We need to get out of here and find people, that's the first priority. But, on our way out, I'll keep my eyes open for food. There's plenty in this forest, I've feasted on wild plants, roots, berries, and more. It'll be okay.

We're going to be okay.

I take his hand and we work our way through the woods.

The undergrowth is thin in this area, the soil is rocky and the hiking isn't too difficult.

"There's a clearing up ahead," I say. It's about a half-mile away. I can just make out the edge of the tree line. Then I hear a sound, a loud whooshing.

"What is that?" I ask.

Sam tilts his head and listens. "I think..." His eyes light up. "That's a helicopter."

We look at each other.

"They're looking for us," I say.

"The clearing," he says.

Then we both start to run. If we can get to the clearing and signal the helicopter we'll be out of here in minutes. No hiking, no flagging down cars. In five minutes this will all be over. I don't know where the last bit of energy comes from, but Sam and I sprint through the woods and charge into the clearing. He reaches it before me. When he does he pulls to a stop. I slam into him and bounce back. He doesn't move. He just stands there.

"What is it?" I ask.

He doesn't say anything. I come around him, then I see why he's stopped. The far edge of the clearing is filled with people.

"What is this?" I ask. He doesn't have to answer. I realize almost right away what it is. They're here for us. It's an organized search. There are the big white tents with tables and chairs. There are water coolers and food.

More than that, there are a dozen news vans with satellite dishes, reporters, and cameramen. Are they all here for us? Are there always so many searchers and reporters for two missing hikers? The helicopter is louder now. It hovers over the clearing, nearer to us than the search party and reporters. The meadow grass flattens under the wind of its beating blades. The helicopter sets down and the blades slow. The engine stops and the clearing grows quiet. The reporters and searchers are looking our way, and then I realize that they've seen us. Because there's a shout, and a cheer, and then dozens of people are running our way.

"What is this?" I ask again. I'm confused. Everything is a blur, a daze.

"Stay with me," Sam says.

"I'm not leaving you," I say.

But the next minute, the most beautiful, long-legged, pouty-lipped woman jumps out of the helicopter and flings herself into Sam's arms. He stumbles back, catches her. She wraps her arms around him and plasters her body against his. I step back, confused. Who...what? Then the woman covers his mouth, not with a happy-to-see-you kiss, but with a let's-make-babies-right-here kiss. A roaring fills my ears and I blink, suddenly dizzy. The reporters have reached us, the cameras.

"Sam?"

A woman grabs me, holds me up. She has a microphone and she shoves it at me.

"You've been lost in the woods with Frederick Knight for five days. An ordeal that most women in America would kill for. How was it? Did he show his legendary charm? What did you do to survive?"

I stare at the reporter, unable to comprehend what she's saying. What she's asking. I shake my head, push the microphone away.

"Sam?" I call. There are a dozen people separating us.

The woman from the helicopter still clings to his arm. But there are other women with him now. A half dozen of them in short, tight dresses, one is in a bikini, like she'd been... sunbathing? They are all kissing him, touching him. The reporters surround him, shout questions at him. He's looking around, I can tell he's agitated.

Then there's a loud shout, and a woman in a sundress pushes through the crowd and throws herself into his arms.

He looks at her, and then clasps her to him. Like he *loves* her.

I turn back to the reporter that asked me the question. There's a whining noise in my ears and black dots dancing in my vision. Sam's...Sam is...

"What did you say?" I ask. My voice is thick and heavy, comes from a far-away place.

"You spent five days lost in the woods with Frederick Knight..."

I don't hear anything else she says. I stare at Sam.

Not Sam.

Frederick.

Not Sam at all.

That man is...

I take in the number of reporters. The media frenzy. The helicopter. The dozen of model-esque women surrounding him.

He's...

I clasp my stomach, bend over, certain I'm about to throw up. Bile rises and I start to gag.

"She needs help," the reporter shouts.

My legs give out and I collapse to the ground. I grab the long grass and try to steady myself. Pull in heaving breaths.

He's not...

Tears swim in my eyes. I look up. Who are these woman?

Does it matter? Frederick Knight always has women surrounding him. Because he's a player.

The King of Players.

The truth slams into me.

I've been played.

Was it just five days ago that I told my friends to never trust a man? That they're all players or wanna-be players? I knew their tactics, *only you understand me, I feel like I've known you forever,* and...

I draw in a ragged breath.

I remember what I always told my friends. Players use the biggest con of all. Right before they lift your skirt they always say...

I love you.

I picture the moment he said I love you, right before he...

A sob escapes me. But...that doesn't make sense. He said his name was Sam. He saved me. He cared...he...

Suddenly, he's there. He drops to the ground in front of me.

"Veronica, are you okay? Talk to me, are you okay?" He pulls me toward him. Looks up at the surrounded crowd and shouts for a paramedic.

I shake my head. I don't need a paramedic.

"You're..." the words stick in my throat. "You're *Frederick Knight.*"

"No," he says. I look around at the reporters pressing in, the women. "I mean yes, but..."

I shake my head. The blood rushes from me and I feel cold.

I look at his face again. The sun is higher and the morning light is bright.

I stare at him and I don't see the man I know. I see... Frederick Knight. I don't know how I missed it before, in the dawning light of the woods. His honey-colored hair, his sharp nose, his full lips, the hazel eyes that wooed a thousand woman. His perfect physique, the muscular shoulders and washboard abs. I recognize him now. I've seen him too often on the front pages of magazines and the news headlines. His is the face that mocked me, the face I ran from.

I'm going to be sick. I gave myself to Frederick Knight. I fell in love with a player.

I think back on my actions with dawning horror. I fell in love with him. I couldn't imagine leaving him in the cave. I couldn't leave him. I was going to die with him rather than save myself.

I became my worst nightmare. I was worse than my mom. At least she had a home and a life, I was going to stay with Frederick Knight in a cave. To die.

"Get away from me," I say.

His face loses color. "My family calls me Sam. I am Sam. To you I'm Sam. Veronica please."

I shake my head. Yank my arms from his.

"Don't touch me," I say. "You lied. You played me."

My heart pounds in my chest and even now, I still want him. I want him to say it's all been a mistake and we'll go home and have a shower and...no. He's made me weak. He's a player. We get out of the woods and the first thing he does is make out with another woman. Even after seeing that, though, I want to stay with him.

He's made me weak.

"Let me explain," he whispers fiercely.

I shake my head no. Tears blur my vision. "You had five days to explain. Remember our pact? No lies, no deceptions, just the truth. No secrets in the cave. You had five days to tell me the truth and you didn't."

He closes his eyes. Nods. "You're right," he says. "I'm sorry."

"You aren't who you said you were," I say. My voice is ragged and I feel an aching, tearing at my heart.

"No. You're right. I'm Frederick Knight," he agrees. "But I love you. I love you more than you can know."

His voice is Sam's, the voice that comforted me and whispered to me and made me feel safe, but it's all wrong because the voice I love is coming from the face of the man I loathe.

Don't I? Don't I loathe him?

He reaches out and takes my hands again. I see the paramedics with a stretcher push their way through the crowd. They're fifty feet away. They'll be here soon. Take me away from here.

Before they do I need to make something clear.

I won't spend my life with a player. I can't. Years of news footage flashes in my mind, Frederick Knight with half-naked women, Frederick Knight walking the red carpet with beautiful actresses, Frederick Knight, this man, in a hot tub pouring champagne over gorgeous models...six days ago.

I won't spend my life in love with a man who will make me weak and break me down. I won't.

It's funny, Miss Erma was right, I couldn't run from fate. I tried, so it threw me in a pit, plunged me in the dark, and had me fall for the man I swore I'd never like, much less love. Frederick Knight may be my soul mate, Miss Erma was right, I couldn't run, but I won't make the mistake my mom did. I won't stay with a liar and a cheat and a player.

"Sam," I whisper.

He nods and a light of hope enters his eyes. My heart responds, wants to latch onto the fact that he says he loves me. But my dad claimed to love my mom too. Players always claim they love you.

"Remember when I promised you that I'd never be with my soul mate?"

"Yes?"

I swallow back tears. "You said you'd never let me fall for my soul mate? You promised me that you'd never let me be with him? Remember?" My voice breaks on the question.

"Yes. Of course I remember. I won't let you. I promise."

He squeezes my hands. I look into his face, remind myself of who he is. The billionaire player with magazine cover good looks. The man with a multitude of lovers and a trail of broken hearts.

"My soul mate is Frederick Knight," I whisper.

He sucks in a breath. Shock and confusion light his eyes.

"But…" He stops, looks at me, and I can't read what his eyes are trying to tell me. Because they are Frederick Knight's eyes, the eyes of a player. A man I don't know.

"If you care about me," I say, "then you'll stay away from me. Out here in the world, you're Frederick Knight, and I never want to see you again."

"Veronica?" His voice is full of shock and…fear?

"No," I say. And it hurts, it hurts so much. "Your story was right, you're Theseus. And I'm Ariadne. I saw the other women. I helped you out of the labyrinth, and now…we'll go our separate ways."

"No. That's not what I want, I want you."

The worst part of this is…I want him too. Even knowing who he is.

Then the paramedics rush to my side, help me to the stretcher. Nick, Chloe's husband, is there and I reach for his hand. Thankful to see someone I know and trust.

"Nick," I say.

"Vee, are you okay? Thank God, you're safe," Nick says.

"Veronica, please." Sam…no, Frederick, says. I have to think of him as Frederick. He rushes forward, tries to reach me.

I close my eyes at the sight of his face. It hurts too much. "Stay away from me," I whisper.

Sam grabs for my hand. His fingers brush against mine and a small sob escapes when I remember all the times he laced his fingers through mine.

I hear a scuffle, then, "Buddy. You heard her. Back off."

That was Nick, former military man, uber-protective of his wife, and apparently also protective of his wife's best friend.

I open my eyes. Nick's back at my side. I'm being loaded into an ambulance.

"Is he...backing off?" I hate that I really hope he says no. That I hope Sam keeps coming. Except...I don't want that.

"Nah, the reporters surrounded him. He couldn't get past them."

I sigh with relief. Suddenly, exhaustion overwhelms me.

"Did he...hurt you?" asks Nick.

"No," I cry. "No. Never." At least not in the way Nick's asking. My hand goes to my heart. "We got lost in a cave. He saved my life. I just...I don't want to see him."

"Then you won't," Nick says.

The paramedic comes close and attaches a blood pressure cuff.

"I'm alright," I say. "It was just...I'm just a little dizzy."

It doesn't matter what I say. They're taking me to the hospital.

They boost me into the back of the ambulance.

Sam, no, Frederick, has been swallowed by a mass of reporters. I wonder if they'll get him to the hospital. He needs fluids, food. Someone needs to make sure his vitals are okay. I stop my line of thought. He's not mine to care about or take care of.

I can see him still trying to push his way through the crowd, to get to me. My chest pinches. He looks up, sees me watching him. Determination fixes on his face. He wants to get to me. He wants...me.

I shake my head. "I want to go now," I say. Then more forcefully, "Now."

"I'll meet you there," Nick says. "Chloe's already in the hospital."

"What? Why?" I look at Nick, and I notice that he looks

exhausted and worried, worried for more than just me. "What is it?"

He takes a deep breath then, "The baby. She came early. They don't know if...they're doing everything they can."

Oh no. Chloe's baby. She's...

I picture Chloe holding my hand over her stomach, the joy in my best friend's eyes every time the baby kicked.

I nod. "I'll see you there," I say.

The doors to the ambulance slam shut.

I clear the past five days from my mind. I wipe Sam from my heart. I push away all the weakness that I feel for him, all the love. I wash it away.

I made it out of the cave alive, I did it. Except, why is it then that I feel less alive than I did when I was with him, sure we were going to die?

I made it out, but I didn't make it out with my heart intact.

Sam is Frederick Knight. Sam is...

Frederick Knight.

14

SAM

Veronica is gone. I fight my way through the reporters. The ambulance lights flash, it pulls out of the clearing onto a service road and drives away.

Dang it.

Another paramedic team makes their way toward me. It's an absolute zoo.

"Frederick. Mr. Knight." The reporters clamor around and shout questions. "Where have you been the last five days?"

"Were you worried for your life?"

"Is it true you and Clara are getting married?"

I flinch at the last question. It was Clara in the helicopter, coming to the search under some misguided attempt at publicity. Apparently she played the grieving girlfriend while I was lost.

"No," I say to the media. "We are *not*."

I pushed her away as soon as possible and told her in no uncertain terms that we were not together. She *knew* that, but she'd wanted to use the press for a career boost.

"Are you and Veronica Diaz dating?" another reporter shouts.

I swing my head toward the reporter that asked the question. I hadn't known Veronica's last name. She would hate these questions. She'd hate being under the scrutiny of reporters and tabloids. Even more, she would hate the insinuation that she's one of many women that I, Frederick Knight, has played.

"No comment," I say in a hard voice.

The paramedics back the reporters away.

"We need to take you to the hospital. Any family here with you?"

"My sister," I say. I point out Evie. She ran to me after I pushed Clara aside. I was so happy to see her. I didn't realize how much until she was hugging me, crying in my arms. She chided me, told me I was an idiot, and that I was never allowed to go hiking again. A pain pinches in the center of my chest.

If Veronica...if she'll have me, I'll be hiking a lot.

We're loaded into the back of the second ambulance.

The sirens blare and the ambulance bounces over the dirt service road.

At the hospital I'm given a thorough exam. Filled with fluids, calories and antibiotics. I'm cleaned up, poked, prodded, x-rayed, bandaged and declared as healthy as can be expected. I don't care. None of it matters. The only thing that matters is finding out where Veronica is. If she's okay.

I keep asking. The nurses, the doctors, the x-ray tech, but no one will tell me anything. It's as if she's disappeared, or...she doesn't want me to see her.

Two hours after I've arrived at the hospital I've had enough.

"Where's Veronica?" I ask the nurse. "I need to see her. Make sure she's okay."

The nurse shakes her head. But she says more than anyone has before, "She's not taking visitors."

My heart pounds in my chest and I close my eyes. She's here. She's here somewhere.

When the nurse leaves the room I turn to my sister.

Her eyebrows are raised and she's watching me with a funny expression on her face.

"Sam, I think...are you..."

"Do not psychoanalyze me, Evie," I warn.

She smiles and her eyes crinkle. "She looked like a nice woman," she says.

My hands clench into fists. "She's not nice," I say.

Evie's forehead wrinkles.

"She's brave and strong and kind and funny and loving and I..." My throat tightens. I take hold of the IV taped to my arm and I slowly pull it out. "I'm going to find her." I pull off the heart rate monitor, the pulse ox, all the ties and cords.

"Okay," she says. "I'll wait here. I'll tell them you're in the bathroom."

"Thanks, Evie."

"Of course."

I hurry from the room. When I see someone coming down the hall I duck my head and turn the opposite direction. It's a small hospital. If I can remain inconspicuous I'll be able to find her room. After a few close calls, some eavesdropping, and blatant lurking, I find her. I grab a newspaper from an empty nurse's station and hold it in front of my face while I stand diagonal to her room. The tall guy, Nick, comes out looking stressed and worried. He strides down the hall. I pray that he's a cousin or a eunuch. Because if he cares about her as much as it looks, and he tries to press his advantage while she's hurting, I...my stomach bottoms out. I imagine she'd choose him over me.

I can't let her do that.

I love her. And I know that she loves me.

I look around. The hall's empty. I step into Veronica's room and close the door.

"Nick?" she asks.

"No, it's me," I say.

She looks up and I think her eyes flare with happiness, although I can't tell because the expression is quickly covered.

"Who's Nick?" I ask. "Are you together?"

She shakes her head. "Nick? No...I...why are you here?"

I sit down next to her. She's hooked up to an IV just like I was. I'm glad they're taking care of her.

"I wanted to explain," I say.

She shakes her head. "I saw you kissing that woman. I know who you are. There's no explaining it away."

"I wasn't. I didn't..." I stop. I realize how lame it sounds. I know what it looked like and it didn't look good. "Please. You said that there weren't supposed to be any secrets in the cave. There weren't. I was myself with you. I was more myself there with you than I have been in years. You *know* me. You do."

"I hate this," she cries. "You sound like Sam, but when I look at you, you're not Sam, you're...*him*." The way she says *him*, with such hurt and fear and disgust, makes me flinch like I've been struck. I look across the room and see my face in the mirror. It's me. Light brown hair, hazel eyes...him. The man on all the covers of magazines and in the news. I turn away from my reflection, look back at Veronica, desperate that she see *me*. Hear me. An idea strikes.

"Close your eyes," I say.

"What?"

"Close your eyes," I say. I nod, urge her to listen.

She looks at me then lets her lids close. I breathe out a sigh of relief.

"It's me," I say. I thread my fingers through hers. Her lips shake. "We made it."

A tear falls down her cheek.

"I'm sorry I didn't tell you who I was. At first, I was scared. So many people only see what the media says about me. Or they see the money or my appearance. They don't look past that. I wanted you to know me, not what other people say or write about me. I was scared that if you knew who I was you would turn away. You would believe the worst of me. And that me being Frederick Knight, in that cave, would hurt our chances of surviving. I wanted to be myself with you. Then after a while I wasn't Frederick Knight anymore. I wasn't even Sam. I was the man who loved you. And that's all I am. The man who loves you."

Her lips tremble and more tears squeeze from her closed eyes.

"I'm sorry I didn't tell you. I can't change my past. But I can be the man you know going forward. I can show you every day that I'm the man you know. The one you fell in love with."

I stop, let go of her hand and reach up to wipe the tears from her cheeks. Rub my thumb over her lip. I want more than anything to settle down next to her and pull her in my arms.

"What do you say?" I ask. "Shower and bed?"

Her eyes open and when she looks at me she flinches. My chest fills with icy dread.

"I'm sorry," she says. "I can't."

"What if I told you that not even a hundredth of what you see in the news about me is true?"

She shakes her head. Holds back a sob.

"I'd be true to you," I promise her. "I'd give you the world. Everything we dreamed of. Italy, New Zealand, sunset in Central Park. I'd give you everything. Heaven on earth. The only catch is, it'd come with me."

I hold out my palm.

"Hold my hand?" I ask.

I wait, holding my breath, praying that she'll reach up and take my hand in hers. The seconds tick by. My chest tightens, my stomach sinks. Long after I know she isn't going to reach up I leave my hand hanging there. Waiting.

She looks at my face, my eyes, my mouth, my hand.

"I'm scared," she whispers. "You...I look at you and..." She stops. "Please."

I don't know what else to say. I don't know how to fix this. My body feels leaden, weighed down and I don't know that I can leave.

She forcefully wipes the tears from her cheeks. Then her shoulders stiffen and she seems to come to a decision. I can tell she doesn't like it, and I won't either, but she's stubborn and I know she's chosen her path.

"Remember when I asked if what we felt in the cave would pass?" she asks.

"Don't," I say, scared of what she's going to say.

"I said that maybe what we felt was because of the situation. The adrenaline and the fear for our lives. That situations like that cause people to feel emotions that don't exist." She sniffs back tears and nods her head.

"No," I say. I ache to pull her in my arms, kiss this idiotic idea from her head.

"Yes. That's what happened," she says. "It wasn't real. None of it was real." She swallows and presses her lips together so tight that they turn pale.

"No," I argue. "You don't mean that."

She looks at me again, then deliberately looks at my face, lets the knowledge of who I am fill her.

"I do mean it," she says. And whether she does or not, I can tell she's made her decision. The stubborn, beautiful, determined woman.

She means it. She's saying goodbye.

My breath rushes out and my ribs ache. I feel trapped in the cave again, unable to break free. The darkness closes around me. I look at my palm, hanging in the air between us. Empty.

I cling to the hope of my last argument. "You claimed that I'm your soul mate," I argue. "You said—"

"That I would never, ever love Frederick Knight."

The darkness that I thought I escaped weighs down on me.

"You'll never love Frederick Knight," I repeat, my voice sounds wooden and hollow.

She watches as I drop my hand. Close my fist around empty air.

"I can't," she says.

This is the same moment as so many that came before. When someone sees me, they reject me. Except, not Veronica. She wouldn't.

"You're scared," I say. "I understand. I'm here. I'm not leaving. We'll do this together, I'm—"

"Goodbye," she whispers. Then, "Goodbye, Frederick."

And the way she says the name Frederick, cold and distant, like she doesn't know me, I understand that this is the end. This really is goodbye.

I think about all the things she told me about her soul mate. Even I thought he was reprehensible. Even I didn't want her to be with him. From her view, and the view of the world, he was a player.

The kind of man that doesn't deserve her.

I understand.

"Goodbye," I say. I brush my fingers over hers. Memorize the feel of her hands. "For what it's worth, thank you. I owe you more than my life."

She drops her head. "You're welcome," she says.

I turn to go, start to walk out.

"Sam?" she says.

I stop. Turn back to her. Pray that she's changed her mind, realized that she's not scared, that she's brave and courageous and...

"Thank you too," she says. She smiles and lifts her hand in farewell.

I nod, my throat too tight to respond. Then I do what I promised never to do. I leave her.

15

VERONICA

I STAND in the hospital's neonatal intensive care unit with Chloe. My goddaughter lays all alone in a bassinet covered in clear plastic. The hospital staff calls it an incubator. There's a door that I can reach through to hold her hand.

"Can I?" I ask Chloe.

I blink my eyes and try to keep back the tears. Chloe doesn't need to see me cry or break down. Her baby was born prematurely and needs oxygen, pulmonary support, nutrition, and more to make it through the next few weeks. Chloe needs a strong friend, not a weepy mess. But when I look at Ava, my goddaughter, all alone in the plastic box, it reminds me of being trapped in the cave. The one thing that got me through it was being able to touch Sam. Just hold his hand. If I had to be alone in a cave, surrounded by walls on all four sides, with no one to touch...no one there, I'd...

"She likes to hold hands," says Chloe. "You can see her heart rate calm when you do." She gives me a watery smile.

"I understand," I say. I'll stay as long as I can. Hold Ava's hand as much as she needs.

"I get to have skin to skin contact too. She lays on my chest and I sing to her. She likes that best. Well, she likes Nick's voice best. He used to sing to her this lullaby and she'd always go to the side of the womb where he sang. Whenever he sings it now, she turns to him and reaches out."

Chloe wipes at her eyes and I pull her close for a quick hug.

"I'm okay," she says. "Just tired."

I reach into the incubator and gently place my pointer finger in Ava's hand. Her hand is small and soft, and she wraps it around my finger. My heart skips a beat at her firm hold.

"She's strong," I say, surprised at the strength of her grip. "Hello, Ava Marie."

"We chose a different name," Chloe says.

I look over at her. "Really?" They'd settled on Ava Marie as soon as Chloe knew she was pregnant.

Chloe nods. "Ava Veronica."

"What?" I shake my head. "Why'd you do that?"

Chloe leans into my side. "The day after you left you didn't answer any texts, then we heard Frederick Knight was missing too. The next day I had the emergency C-section and you still didn't answer. I knew something was wrong. You would've come if you'd known. Nothing would've stopped you from coming."

I reach over and clutch her arm.

"So, I realized you were in trouble. But I also knew that you're the most kick-butt, bravest, strongest woman I know. You'd get out of whatever trouble you were in. When Ava was born too early to breathe without help, and I realized she was going to have to fight for her life, I wanted her to fight. To be brave. To be like you. Fearless."

Tears fall from my eyes and I wipe them away.

I think of how I was the exact opposite of fearless with Sam. I'm so scared of what might happen, of him being Frederick

Knight, that I rejected him, full stop. I ran. Just like I've been doing from the first. I'm not brave at all.

"She will," I say. "She'll get out of here."

Chloe wraps her arm around my waist and leans her head on my shoulder. "I know," she says. "She has a lot to look forward to. A daddy who adores her. A mom who loves her to bits."

"A godmother who is going to spoil her rotten." I smile. "It's going to be okay," I say. "I'm here. Anything you need."

"I've been illustrating like crazy since Ava was born. I've got an idea for a preemie line, NICU crib art," she says.

I look at the picture on the crib. It's a drawing of a cat, a dog, and a baby bird and it says *Be brave, little one.*

"Good idea," I say. "I'll take care of everything at work. You take as much time as you need."

I've only had a day of recovery, fluids, food and rest. I'm still exhausted, but I'm ready to move on and get back to work.

The thought, *you're running away,* flashes through my mind.

"Thank you," says Chloe. "What did I do to deserve a friend like you?"

I tilt my head, try to lighten the mood. "I don't know, I think it was when we were three and you shared your juice box with me. Or it could've been when you let me dress your Barbies in tomboy clothes and take them on hikes."

We sit quietly for a moment. I think about how twenty-five years ago, I never would've guessed that Chloe and I would be sitting here together. I wiggle my finger and Ava's grip tightens on my hand. She has dark, nearly black hair, just like Nick's, but her rosebud mouth is a replica of Chloe's.

"I love her already," I say.

Chloe nods. Then she smooths her hands over her dress. I smile, leave it to Chloe to be four days post-delivery and dressed in a lacy yellow sundress with her curly hair barely restrained by a matching yellow scarf. I look down. I'm in my usual too. Khaki shorts, a tank top, hiking boots. Chloe calls it my Tomb Raider look. We're quite a pair.

Opposites in nearly every way, except for one thing—how much we care about each other.

My mind turns back to Sam. The world would see us as opposites too, but...

Last night, while I was sleeping, something woke me up. The room was pitch black. I didn't know where I was, I thought for a moment I was still in the cave. Half-asleep, confused and scared, I reached over and tried to find Sam. For thirty seconds I scrambled over the bed, flinging my hands about, searching for him. My heart beat in my ears because I couldn't find him. Then, my mind cleared and I realized I wasn't in the cave, I was in bed, and Sam wasn't with me anymore.

I wonder how many times I'll wake up in the dark expecting to feel him next to me.

"Veronica?" asks Chloe.

"Yeah?"

"You fell in love with him, didn't you?"

My shoulders drop and I watch the rise and fall of Ava's breaths. I should've known that Chloe would address this. She may be a new mom with a baby in the NICU, but she's still my best friend, and the world's biggest romantic. She'll want to make sure I'm okay.

"Don't worry about it," I say. "You just need to concentrate on Ava."

"Does he deserve you?" she asks. "I want to know if he's a good enough guy for my best friend. If not, Nick's company is doing really well, he can send one of his guys over to pull a rough up job."

I laugh. "I thought Nick had a security company. Not the

mafia. What's wrong with you?" I laugh at the wicked glint in her eyes.

"Well, you once offered to tie Nick up and dump him in the woods if he hurt me. I thought I'd return the favor."

"In my defense, that's before I realized Nick is actually a hard shell with a gooey, soft center."

"And so is Frederick Knight? He's not actually a player?" she asks hopefully.

I fiddle with the drawstring on my shorts, not sure how to answer her question. "I don't know," I say. "When we were in the cave together, I would've bet my life that he wasn't. But I don't know how to reconcile that with how the media portrays him."

She nods, "You'll figure it out."

With reluctance I pull my hand from Ava's grasp. She waves her arm, like she's trying to reach me.

"I'll see you soon," I say to Chloe. I put my hand on the plastic of the incubator. "Bye, baby girl."

Be brave.

Six weeks later, my life is back into a semi-normal routine. I visit Chloe and Ava at the hospital in the mornings. Ava is getting stronger every day, and the doctors say she could go home soon. I bring Chloe a caramel latte and pick up any illustration concepts she's conceived, and then I update her on the freelancers covering the creative aspects of the company. I'm going to have to implement the plan Sam and I came up with to expand staffing. Our business has grown far beyond the capabilities of two partners and a couple freelancers.

All my bruises and scrapes have healed. I'm rested and have

completely regained my strength. The only thing that hasn't healed is the hollow ache in my chest. It's as if a part of me has been cut out and I don't have the piece needed to fill the emptiness.

I still wake up in the dark expecting to find Sam there. When he's not, I make myself close my eyes, breathe deep and fall back asleep.

The reporters left town long ago. After a few days of hounding me for an interview they gave up, packed into their vans, and went in search of more salacious news.

Sometimes I see Frederick Knight on the TV. But it's old pictures, old footage, and they're speculating about what he's doing now, who he's seeing, where he is. Why he's been out of the limelight for more than a month. No one has seen him since the clearing and he's not giving interviews. For a few weeks they played the footage of him in the clearing. They loved to zoom in on his bruised face as a reporter shouts, "Are you and Veronica Diaz dating?" and then he swings to the camera, his expression bordering on violence as he snarls, "No comment." The tabloids and entertainment industry loved dissecting that clip. Most finally agreed that The King of Players and the "hiker woman" had nothing between them but survival.

After watching weeks of news about him, I realized that the woman he hugged as if he loved her was his sister. And I know from what he told me that he does love her, they're a close-knit family and they care about each other. The woman in the helicopter was an ex-girlfriend, angling for a media spotlight. What I saw wasn't what I thought it was.

Every time an image of him comes on TV, or I see a picture of him in a tabloid, I don't feel scared anymore. Before when I realized who he was and saw his face, I was terrified. Now, when I see a picture of him in a tuxedo, or on a yacht, or climbing down from a helicopter, I try to see his eyes. I try to see *him*. To see the truth.

So now, when I see pictures of Frederick Knight, I look for the truth. I look for him.

I walk down Appleseed Court, the street I grew up on. I step over a large crack in the sidewalk. The same crack my bike tire used to hit every time I rode to and from school. I look at the colonial house in front of me. It's painted light bluish gray, with red shutters. The flower beds need weeding, but the grass is trimmed. I stand at the edge of the lawn and put my hands in my pockets. The light in the kitchen is on and I can see my mom through the window. She's at the kitchen sink washing dishes.

A sprinkler comes on at the neighbors' and a dog barks. I rock back on my heels. My feet itch to turn around and walk back to my car. It's been ten years.

But I'd promised Sam, I'd promised myself that I was going to talk to my mom. When I thought that I was going to die, there were only a few things I'd wanted. To see my mom, to meet my goddaughter, and to meet Sam in the outside world. That hollow spot in my chest clenches. I've met my goddaughter, now it's time to see my mom.

I walk up the sidewalk to the front door. It's painted dark blue now. The last time I was here it was white. There are new ceramic flower pots holding bushy plants and bright flowers. It's familiar, but different. Ten years is a long time, plenty more than flower pots and door colors can change.

I ring the doorbell and then put my hands behind my back.

What will she think? What will she say? Will she even want to talk to me? The last time we spoke I said some ugly things. I told her that she was the weakest, most cowardly woman I knew and that I hoped I was never like her, letting love make me weak. I was eighteen and so sure I knew everything there was to know about the world.

I hear her footsteps on the wood floor, and there's a funny feeling in my stomach and I realize it's fear.

The door swings open. "May I help—" My mom stops, she drops the dish towel in her hand, stares at me in shock.

She's older. Somehow, I never thought that she'd look any different than I remembered her. I never thought she'd age. She has gray hair now and there are lines on her forehead.

"Mom," I say. "I'm sorry."

Then she cries out and rushes to me and pulls me in her arms. She's crying and hugging me. And I throw my arms around her and all that fear that she'd be upset or not want to see me vanishes. All those years of blaming her, trying not to be like her, they fall away. Even the shame of holding it all against her, it falls away as she squeezes me to her.

"I was so worried," she says. "I was so scared for you. My strong girl. My fierce-hearted daughter."

She pulls back and takes my face in her hands. Tears fill her eyes.

"Oh Mom," I say. "I'm sorry for blaming you. I..."

"Come inside," she says. She pulls me into the house. In minutes I'm settled on the living room couch, and my mom brings out a dish of fresh cinnamon rolls and two mugs of coffee.

"Your favorite, extra frosting," she says as she dishes out the cinnamon roll onto a plate and pushes it to me.

I take a sip of coffee. My mom watches me like I'm about to disappear again and she won't see me for another ten years. I feel so stupid. So...wrong. I ran from Sam, but I've been running from my family for ten years. I thought I was brave and strong, people said I was, but when it comes down to it, I'm not. I've been a coward.

"I was at the search," my mom says. She runs her fingers over the handle of her fork.

"You were?" I didn't see her there.

She nods. "As soon as it was organized I was out there looking for you. Praying. I saw you come back, I made sure you were okay. Then I left. I didn't think you'd want to see me there."

I close my eyes against the sting of her words. Then I choose to face them. I've acted poorly.

"I would have," I say.

She looks up in surprise.

"When I was lost, I realized that the one thing in my life that I wished I'd done was tell you that..." I pause and she looks up.

"Yes?"

"That I love you," I say.

She wipes at the tears in her eyes. "I know," she says. "I love you too."

I think about how much Chloe loves her daughter and I can now see that love in my mom.

"I'm sorry for blaming you for staying with Dad. I know that you loved him and sometimes it's hard to leave people you love, even when they hurt you—"

"Veronica," she interrupts.

"What?"

"I didn't stay with your father for love," she says.

"You didn't?"

She shakes her head. "I tried to divorce him when you were three years old."

"What? I didn't know this. Why didn't you tell me?"

She sighs and looks down at her hands twisting in her lap. "I wanted you to have a happy childhood. To feel loved."

"But..." I don't understand.

"Your father had more power than me. More money, more prestige, more connections. He promised that he would take full custody of you and make it so that I would never see you again. That I would never see you, the daughter I loved, if I dared divorce him."

Her words fall like jagged rocks and all my ideas of the past are shattered. One thing is clear.

"You stayed with him for me?"

She nods.

"Why didn't you tell me?" I cry.

"I didn't want you to think poorly of him. Or to feel bad for me. That's too much for a child to carry. I had you, a home, a life. I didn't want you to think that you were the cause of any unhappiness. Or to think that I regretted my choices. I never regretted them. The pain of marriage, your father's cheating, I'd do it all over again. Because I got you."

"But I blamed you," I cry. "I didn't speak to you for ten years."

She nods. "I should've told you. After his funeral, after our argument. But I was scared. I didn't want you to think I was weak for staying with him. You wouldn't have let yourself be bullied. I see how you've grown up and I'm so proud of you."

"No, that's not true," I say. I think of how much courage she had to stay in a marriage full of betrayal. How much strength she had to face each day so that she could stay in my life. I can't imagine how much worse my childhood would've been if my dad were actually a single parent. I would've been his player-bait for years longer. "I don't think you're a coward at all. I think you're strong."

All these years I thought that my mom was made weak through loving my dad. I thought she stayed with him *because* she was weak. But that wasn't it at all. She stayed with him for me. And loving me made her strong enough to do that.

Love made her strong.

I've been so wrong. About everything. All my life there have been instances of love making people strong. My mom. Chloe and Nick. Ava. Sam and me. I don't think that we would've survived the cave without the love we felt for each other.

I've been so blind.

Sam knew too. He asked me to stay with him, to trust him, and I couldn't. My throat tightens. What if he's moved on? Written me off? I told him that I could never love Frederick Knight. And he...believed me?

In the cave, he did tell the truth. He loved me, let me see the real him, chanced rejection, something he feared, and I let him down. I'm ashamed of myself. It's hard to see all the things that I've done wrong and all the ways I've hurt people and let them down.

"Can you forgive me?" I ask through the lump in my throat. "I've been...horrid."

"No," she cries. She reaches out and takes my hands. "Horrid people refuse to grow. They don't acknowledge faults. They stay stuck in the past and refuse to change. You're not horrid. You only needed some time to grow. That's called being human."

I curl into my mom and thank the universe, or fate, or whatever it was that led me to falling into that cave. Because it led me back to my mom. And it gave me Sam.

I hope. I hope it gave me Sam.

"You're really wise, Mom," I say.

She shrugs. "Took me sixty years and a lot of pain and mistakes to get here. Mistakes and pain are the best fertilizer for growth."

I smile at her and she smiles back. I feel warm inside and happy. I didn't realize how much not talking with my mom had hurt me. How much I'd been hurting myself.

The realization fills me.

I can't keep making this same mistake.

I jump up from the couch.

"I'll be back," I say, "but I need to go. I need to go right now." I hurry to the door.

There's an urgency in me. I have to go see Sam. I can't run away any more. I have to see him now. I have to tell him how I feel. Beg him to forgive me for letting him down. I see *him*. I do.

"Where are you going?" my mom calls after me, surprise filling her voice.

I turn, my hand on the door handle.

"To see about the rest of my life."

Then I run out the door and down the sidewalk, jump into my car. I'm not afraid anymore. I'm not running away. I'm running forward. To Sam. To meet him in the outside world.

FIVE HOURS LATER I STAND OUTSIDE FREDERICK KNIGHT'S offices on a quiet street in Tribeca. I'm actually surprised at how quiet the street is. There isn't a single person besides me on the sidewalks. I always thought every street in New York was constantly bustling, but that's not really the case. There are people on the busy cross street a block down, but here, it's quiet.

His office is a six-story building, built circa the 1880s, with a brown sandstone exterior.

He's on the top floor. I know this because the stainless steel placard next to the security desk told me so. Unfortunately, the security officer also told me that I'm not welcome in the building. Unauthorized visitors are prohibited, and he wouldn't break protocol and call up to Mr. Knight's offices to check if I could be admitted.

Why would he? I'm in camo shorts, a white tank top, and hiking boots. My hair is down and wind-blown and there's a sheen of sweet coating my forehead. I'm way out of place compared to the sleek-haired, business-suited, flashy types I saw as I searched for parking.

I probably look like a crazy Frederick Knight groupie aiming for a hookup, or some country bumpkin on a field trip trying to gain admittance to see a billionaire. Or a con artist. He may have thought I was a con artist.

"Please, just call up. He'll want to see me. I guarantee it," I said.

The security guard looked me over. *"That's what they all say," he said. "Sorry, ma'am. Please exit the building. Mr. Knight does not receive visitors. Ever."*

And that was that.

I did manage to learn that he comes in and out of the building through a private entrance and that his driver waits at the door. The private entrance isn't accessible to the public. I read that tidbit after a quick search on my phone while standing outside this building. It's on a fan girl blog devoted to Frederick Knight sightings. Apparently, women used to stake out his offices, but gave up after they realized he never used the front door and was never seen on the sidewalk. But thanks to the blog I also know that his desk is in the west-facing corner office of the sixth floor. I crane my neck. The window has a nice eight-inch ledge and... I smile to myself. His window is cracked open. A few inches, but still, that's enough.

My car, parked down the street, had all my climbing gear in the trunk. I have on my climbing shoes, my chalk bag, and holy crap...I'm going to free climb a six-story building.

I let out a shaky breath. It's alright. I've got this.

Sam and I climbed worse in the cave, in the dark. There was no safety net then either.

I stare up at the building. Trace my route. There are plenty of holds and ledges, and if I get stuck there's scaffolding set up against the building next door.

I don't know how else to get in contact with Sam. I don't have his number. His business phone isn't listed. I don't have his email. I don't know his address. It's not like we exchanged contact information in the cave. Celebrity billionaires are surprisingly difficult to contact. The security guard at the desk wouldn't take a message to relay. I could wait and see if he comes back to Romeo, but wait for how long? He hasn't been back in six weeks.

I swing my arms back and forth, stretching them out. I stretch my legs.

A memory flashes in my mind. I was fifty feet up, Chloe was belaying and Erma was trying to tell me the name of my soul mate. I was climbing as fast as I could to get away from him.

I walk up to the building and boost myself onto the rough stone of the wall.

Then I start the slow, careful climb up.

To Sam.

16

SAM

It's been forty-four days since I left. The same number as the depth of the pit that Veronica nearly fell in. I push the thought away. Concentrating on the past doesn't help me. For the last six weeks I've been looking toward the future. Planning, building, being the man that I know I am.

"We're all set," I say. "I look forward to working with you."

"Thank you, Mr. Knight. Me as well," says Kyle Davidson, a passionate, driven PhD and my newest hire, the soon-to-be Head of Research and Development at Knight Research Laboratories. "And may I say," says Kyle, "I believe wholeheartedly in your mission and I respect you immensely. You aren't at all like what they—" He drops off and clears his throat. "I mean...thank you for the position. I look forward to overseeing our research." I can see on the video chat his cheeks redden slightly.

I hold back a smile. Kyle Davidson is one of more than two dozen hires I've made in the past month. I chose him as Head of Research and Development because of his candor, and because he was one of the youngest and most brilliant PhDs to come out of MIT in the last decade. He was working at an underfunded academic position scrambling for grant money until I lured him away. It only took the promise of using science and technology for the betterment of humanity in any way that our team could dream up. With one condition, our first project must be developing a prototype search and rescue rover.

"Kyle," I say, "as you're going to be my Head of Research and Development, I need you to feel comfortable being honest with me. I don't need pandering, I need someone to tell me the truth. There's no need to step around my feelings. If we want this project to succeed then I need honesty. Tell me when something works, when it doesn't. I give you leave to be upfront with me. At all times."

Kyle nods and clears his throat again. "In that case," he says, "you aren't at all like I was led to believe. You're driven, you're probably more intelligent than I am, which is hard to accomplish, and I think that you're going to achieve great things. And I look forward to doing that with you."

"Good enough," I say.

We hang up and I lean back in my office chair. I put my hands behind my head, close my eyes and let out a long sigh. I'm in my Tribeca office. The same place I've been nearly eighteen hours every day since I got back to the city. I've been working day and night to put together the business Veronica and I dreamed up in the cave. It's scheduled to begin operations in less than two months. I found a space just outside Romeo that I'm ready to make an offer on. My hires expect to be relocating to Upstate New York. I sigh. What will Veronica think when I start running my business from her hometown?

It's taking a gamble, one that I'm not sure will pay off.

When I left, I wanted to turn around. Within ten feet of leaving her hospital room, I wanted to turn around. But what she said hit home.

Six days before, I had been cavorting with models, donning my player persona. I'd spent five years building that image and I needed to take some time tearing it down. I needed to start, at that very moment, being the man I knew I was. Becoming someone worthy of myself again and through that becoming worthy of her.

She may be afraid of players. She has a right to be, her father pulled a number on her. But she doesn't have to be afraid of me.

I should've told her who I was while we were in the cave. But I realized something important. In the cave I couldn't tell her who I was because I still hadn't accepted me for *me*. And if I couldn't accept myself, how could I expect her to?

So, I accept me. Just as I am. A man who felt unworthy, then was betrayed, then made mistakes, tried to bury pain in the wrong way, and then came out of it again. I accept all of it, the good and the bad.

Instead of turning around and going back to her, I decide to keep moving forward. Building a life I'm proud of.

I lean forward and pick up the phone. I dial the architect firm overseeing the renovations to the house in Romeo.

"How's progress?" I ask without preamble. Dean isn't one for small talk.

"The climbing wall's finished," he says. "I thought you were crazy to ask for it. But I have to say, she looks good."

"Send a picture," I say.

My phone vibrates and I pull up a photo of the room. The corner of my mouth lifts as I stare at the image. The wall looks like rock, but has various routes, holds, and technically complex spots to keep a rock climbing lover busy for years. It's exactly what I wanted.

"It's perfect," I say. Before we end the conversation, he promises that the house will be finished on schedule.

I look at the photograph of the climbing wall and wonder what Veronica would say. Every day, at least ten times every hour, I think of getting up, walking to my car and driving up to Romeo. Evie, in her tendency to psychoanalyze everyone, tells me that I'm suffering from a condition called...love. I tell her to stuff it. She thinks I should go up to Romeo and woo Veronica with all the charm and suavity I have. That's exactly the opposite of what Veronica would want, so I tell Evie I'm handling it.

Except, at times like this, when all I want is to see Veronica, talk to her, hear her voice, touch her...I'm not sure I am handling it.

I'll keep on my course though. I'll start the think tank, get it up and running. I'll renovate the home that we dreamed of together. I stay out of the media spotlight, grateful to move beyond the parties and wastefulness. I'm back working behind a computer on projects I'm proud of. I spend Sunday afternoons with my parents and my sister. My mom and dad came back early from South Africa when they heard I was missing. They haven't said anything, but I know they're relieved that I'm back to being the son they knew. I sent a baby gift to my ex-business partner and ex-wife. I feel nothing but thanks to them. Without their betrayal I would never have met Veronica. I've moved out of the past. In less than two months, Knight Research Laboratories will open in Romeo. The house will be finished.

And I'll ask Veronica...I'll ask her if she'd like to meet me in the outside world.

It's the waiting that's hard.

I drop my head in my hands.

I miss her.

I rub my eyes. I miss her so much. The feel of her hand in mine, her fingers laced and holding on to me tightly. The sound of her soft breath while she sleeps. The feel of her body wrapped in my arms. The sound of her voice. Her sense of humor and her determination. How much she cares—for her friends, her business. How much she cared for me.

I think back to the night we thought all was lost. When we made love. I've never in my life felt so whole and like the world was full of so much light and hope, even though we were lost in the dark. She was a guiding star. Even now she's guiding my actions. I'm becoming the best man I can be.

But I miss her. So much.

Then, I hear a noise. A strange scratching sound, then a knock.

I look up at the door. The knock sounds again. It's not at the door though. It sounds like a knock on glass. From behind me. On the window.

I turn around.

I shake my head. Stare in shock.

Veronica's hands shake on the window ledge and she holds herself against the exterior of the building.

I swear and rush to the window. Yank it up and open. I look down. She's climbed without a harness sixty feet up the side of my office building. Sweat drips down her forehead, her hair tangles in the wind. She blinks at me and gives a cautious smile.

"Hi," she says. Her arms shake on the ledge.

I grab her and pull her into my office. She lands with a soft thud on the hardwood. I notice her climbing shoes. There's chalk on her hands and smudges of chalk on her face. I've never seen a more beautiful sight in my life.

I never knew how much I would love the sight of a woman in climbing gear and hiking shorts.

I want to grab her, kiss her, make love to her. But instead what comes out is, "What are you doing?"

17

I give Sam a hesitant smile. I didn't really have a plan for what I'd do or say after I climbed into his office. About three-quarters of the way up I was just praying that he'd actually be *in* his office.

I take in the sight of him. I've never seen him in person looking like this. In the clearing, and even in the hospital, he was still covered in bruises and cuts, dirt, he had a beard and messy hair. The full effect of him as Frederick Knight wasn't there. Now...it is.

He's in a *man of New York* kind of outfit. Tailored and expensive. His hair is trimmed perfectly and he's close shaven. All the bruises and scrapes have healed. The swelling is gone. He looks just like the man from the magazine covers. A thick lower lip, long eyelashes, a firm jaw, eyes that are made for seduction. Wide shoulders and defined muscles you can see even through his shirt. For a moment, the fear comes back and he looks like a stranger again. A billionaire player that seduces models and actresses and pours champagne on women in hot tubs.

Then I look closer. See the expression in his eyes.

He's looking at me like I'm the only light in the darkest night. Like I'm the first star he's seen and he's making his heart's greatest wish.

I step forward, move toward this man that looks like...like the man who loves me. And the man that I love.

He reaches out, then drops his hands, closes them into fists. I see on his wrist the watch that he wore in the cave. The one he gave me so I could find my way out. He wanted me to live. Even if it meant he'd die alone. Seeing that watch fills me with determination. This is right. I'm not afraid anymore.

"What are you doing?" he asks.

I look into his eyes. They've shuttered and I think he's concerned that somehow I'm going to reject him or hurt him again. Or maybe I was mistaken and it wasn't love I saw. That he's written me off and that's why he hasn't pulled me into his arms.

I'm shaking and I can't tell if it's because my muscles are fatigued or because I'm scared that he's going to ask me to leave. But I can't stop now. I have to move forward. I pray he wants to move forward with me.

"What are you doing?" he asks again, and my heart squeezes at the way he says it. Questioning, cautious, without the love in his voice that I remember.

"Oh," I say and I shrug, determined to keep going. "You know. Just hanging out."

I bite my bottom lip and silently push him to remember.

His brow lowers and he looks confused. Then his eyes clear and the beginnings of a smile forms on his lips.

"Oh yeah?" he asks.

"Yup. Just hanging out. In the outside world."

His eyes turn from hazel to a clear happy green. And a place deep inside me responds to his look and unfurls with shining joy.

"I'm Veronica Diaz," I say. I hold out my hand.

His eyes crinkle and he steps forward, takes my hand in his. I feel his touch to the depths of my soul. I draw in a ragged breath. He looks at me and I can tell that he feels it too.

"Nice to meet you," he says, still holding my hand. Then, "I'm Frederick Knight."

He gives a half-smile and my heart breaks for him. At the way he says his name and the way he looks at me when he does, like he's asking me to accept him.

"Nice to meet you, Frederick," I say.

He lets out a shaky breath. "My friends call me Sam," he says. And the man he was and the man he is come together and I see him just as he is.

"Sam," I repeat.

We stand for a moment just looking at each other. I drink him in, the feel of his hand in mine. This is right.

Then he drops my hand and puts both his hands in his pockets.

I frown at the chill I feel when he lets go.

"Well..." I say, and then I swallow down the lump in my throat. I just want to throw myself in his arms and never let go.

"Well," he repeats.

He looks around his office. I do too. It's large. There's a glass and chrome desk, leather chairs, a seating area with a couch, a mini-bar. The only noise is the ticking of the clock on the wall.

I nod. "Well..." I start again.

"I was wondering," he says. He pauses. I watch as he swallows nervously, then, "You see, you just popped in and the second I saw you...I realized that you're special and that I've never felt this way about anyone before and I wondered if you'd go to dinner with me?" He smiles at me and the corners of his eyes crinkle.

My heart turns over. He's asking me.

I smile at him, and say, "No. No, thank you."

He wipes the expression from his face. Looks at me in silence and doesn't say anything at all.

Maybe I made a mistake, maybe he wasn't going where I thought he was, wasn't replaying the meeting we'd dreamed up. Was I wrong?

I watch the second hand of the stainless steel clock on the wall. I count ten seconds, fifteen, twenty, the whole while I pray...*please remember, please remember.* I'm about to say something, tell him I will, that I'll go to dinner with him, I'll go anywhere with him, when he turns around and strides out of his office.

The door shuts with a hard click.

He...left?

I let out a painful gasp and bend forward. I wrap my arms around my waist. He left. He left me. I grasp my waist and try to pull back the hurt, the shock, the...he didn't remember. I made a mistake.

He left.

My coming here was a mistake.

I take a deep gasping breath, pull back the tears threatening and stand up straight. Wipe away a stray tear that escaped. I turn and look out the window. Walk to it and glance down. Should I climb back down or go out the office door? I think, since Sam didn't say goodbye, he doesn't want to see me again. I close my eyes and forcefully wipe away the tears that are falling freely.

I really messed up.

I turn to the door. I'll walk out through the lobby. I can't stay here any longer. I start for the door when it flings open. Sam rushes in then stops short when he sees me.

"You're crying?"

I shake my head and wipe my eyes. "No," I say.

He kicks the door shut. Then, I notice what he's holding in his hands. Flowers. Pink roses, daisies, lavender, greenery, all mixed together in a beautiful bouquet.

He remembered.

I feel like the sun has come out and it's shining down on me. I smile at him.

He looks down at the water dripping from the stems to the hardwood floor. "I'm sorry. I got them from reception. I didn't have flowers with me...I..."

He holds them out to me. I take them and pull them to my chest. I bury my nose to them and smile into the roses.

"They're perfect," I whisper.

He nods. "I was wondering," he says, "if you'd like to go to Central Park, we'll climb the boulders, then, we could get coffee and cookies at this old Hungarian bakery near where I grew up. Tonight I can take you home and make you pasta. We'll eat it on the roof deck, have wine, and watch the sun set over the river."

I clasp the flowers and feel my heart swell.

He looks at me and nods. He watches as I bite my bottom lip.

"No, I don't think so," I say with a bright smile.

He smiles back. And then I feel it, the hope, the bright shining love that we have for each other.

"No?" he asks with a grin.

"No," I say. "Get lost."

"How about we go to Italy and climb the Dolomites? I'll take you to a villa with a patio and an outdoor oven, we'll drink

Italian wine, and eat olives and fresh bread. I have a private jet, we could be there early tomorrow."

I shake my head. "No. Leave me alone," I say.

He nods. And we look at each other and share that same look we had when we made it out of the cave. Like we can take on the world and do anything as long as we're together.

"Then how about..." He pauses and looks at me with a smile.

"Yes?" I ask, then I hold my breath.

"We could go on a walk?" he asks.

I let my breath out in a rush, start to breathe normally again.

I nod, urge him on.

He steps forward. "I'll be me, and you'll be you, and we'll just walk. Together."

He puts his hand gently to my cheek.

My heart leaps. I turn my head and press my lips into his palm.

"Together?"

He nods.

"Where would we go?" I ask.

"Wherever you like."

"But we'd do it together?"

"That's right."

He strokes his thumb over my lips and I look into his eyes. They shine bright with love.

"How long is this walk?" I whisper.

His hand stills on me and he looks at me with all the hope in the world. "Long," he says. "It starts right now and it goes on for the rest of our lives."

"That sounds nice," I say.

Then I drop the flowers and fling myself into his arms.

He grabs me, pulls me to him and captures my mouth with

his. He buries his hands in my hair and kisses me. Then he pulls away. "I love you," he says fiercely. I don't have time to answer because he's kissing me again. I'm pulling at his pants and he's lifting my shirt. Soon, we're naked. Bare to each other in the daylight.

"My word," he says. "You're beautiful."

"I love you," I say. "I love you so much."

I drop to the couch in the corner of his office and he kneels over me. I run my hands over him, and he touches me reverently, strokes me everywhere. Then he covers my mouth with his and settles inside me. I cry out and he catches my cry with his mouth.

This. This I recognize. This I know.

He starts a rhythm that I remember. I move up to meet him and he moves forward to meet me. He pulls away and then comes back. I pull back and rock forward.

I grasp his shoulders, wrap my legs over his back, hang on as he pushes me higher.

He threads a hand through mine and sends his other hand into my hair. I tilt my chin up and capture his gaze. We stare into each other's eyes as we rock back and forth.

"I see you," I say.

"I know you," he says.

"I love you," I say.

I feel him thicken, pulse inside me, I feel the heat of him coming into me.

"I love you," he says. "I love you."

The sound of his voice, the look in his eyes, the feel of him inside me, it's too much. I cry out, clench around him, the room, already bright, flashes with light. I grasp him, pull him to me and feel our hearts beat against each other as we fall down from the heights of the stars.

He's still smiling into my eyes when my breathing slows and

my heartbeat calms. He places a kiss on the tip of my nose, and over each eyebrow, then a sweet long kiss on my lips.

"I could get used to this," I say.

"You better," he says. Then he turns on his side and wraps me in his arms. We lay together and memorize the feel of each other again. After a few hours and a few more rounds of lovemaking, we slip back into our clothing.

"What now?" I ask.

He smiles and holds out his hand. I take it.

"How about a walk in Central Park, some coffee and cookies from a Hungarian bakery I know?"

He stands and I step into his arms.

"Mmm. That sounds nice. And then how about we have pasta and wine on the roof?"

"And then?" he asks.

I shrug. "Shower and bed?"

A spark enters his eyes and I can tell that he's thinking about skipping the walk and bakery and dinner and going straight to shower and bed.

I grin up at him.

"I'm going to marry you," he says. "You know that, right?"

Happiness blossoms in me, pure and light. I look down at our linked hands and I thank the twist of fate that brought us together.

"Good." I smile up at him, the man I love. "Let's go for that walk."

EPILOGUE
SAM

Sooner rather than later...

The sun spills over the green hills of the Italian olive grove. Veronica lays in my arms in the shade of an olive tree. Bees drone overhead and clouds float lazily in the deep blue Tuscan sky. A picnic basket sits in the grass next us. It's empty of the bread, olives, fresh cheese and wine that we packed earlier. I stroke my fingers through Veronica's hair and kiss the edge of her mouth. Then, I stretch back on the soft picnic blanket, gather her close, and smile up at the light filtering through the leaves.

"Do you think," she asks, "we could do that again?"

I smile. Making love under an olive tree in the Italian sun has its appeal.

"If we hurry," I say. I look at the height of the sun overhead, then at my watch. "Everyone should be here in thirty minutes."

Two weeks ago, Veronica and I were married in a sunrise ceremony in the Dolomites. We flew everyone over to celebrate our wedding with us—my family, Veronica's mom, Chloe, Nick and Ava, and Chloe's Aunt Erma. Ava, a healthy and happy baby, was the flower girl. I think Chloe spent the entire wedding trying to keep Ava from putting rose petals in her mouth.

"That soon?" asks Veronica. She looks at the long empty drive and the quiet countryside road. Between us and the road is the private seventeenth century villa we're staying in. It's a sun-washed yellow with a bright tile roof. There are gardens, an outdoor kitchen and a swimming pool.

We hiked and climbed the Dolomites for the week after our wedding and then took a meandering drive down the coast, exploring villages, wineries and stopping in quite a few empty fields for an hour or two of lovemaking in the sweet grass and sunshine.

Life is better than anything I could ever have imagined.

"Yup. That soon," I say.

Our family and friends explored Italy on their own and are joining us for one last evening before heading back to New York. Veronica and I are going to spend another week in the villa. Hopefully, right under this olive tree.

Veronica starts to run her hand across my bare skin, down my abs, and then she whispers a suggestion in my ear. I glance at her in surprise and there's that look in her eyes, the one that she has when she's planning something especially adventurous.

I swallow. I've never been able to resist that look.

"Come to think of it," I say slowly. "We have plenty of time."

She smiles and I grin back.

"That's what I thought," she says.

I roll her beneath me and get busy fulfilling every whispered request. After we're done and she's back in my arms, sprawled on the blanket, looking up at the sun-drenched sky, I lean over and press my lips to hers.

SAM PRESSES HIS LIPS TO MINE AND I THINK ABOUT HOW LUCKY I am. How loved.

Our family will be here soon, but I want one more minute just taking in the feel of him and the warmth of his lips against mine.

Laying in the Italian sun, wrapped in his arms, I know two things. Love makes you strong and life's an adventure. And adventures are always better when you take them with someone you love.

THE END

GET A BONUS EPILOGUE

Want more Veronica and Sam? Get an exclusive bonus epilogue for newsletter subscribers only.

When you join the Sarah Ready Newsletter you get access to sneak peaks, insider updates, exclusive bonus scenes and more.

Join Today!

www.sarahready.com/newsletter

ALSO BY SARAH READY

Stand Alone Romances:

Hero Ever After

The Fall in Love Checklist

Soul mates in Romeo Series:

Chasing Romeo

Love Not at First Sight

Find more books by Sarah Ready at:

www.sarahready.com/romance-books

ABOUT THE AUTHOR

Author Sarah Ready writes contemporary romance and romantic comedy. Her books have been described as "euphoric", "heartwarming" and "laugh out loud". Her debut novel *The Fall in Love Checklist* was hailed as "the unicorn read of 2020".

Before writing romance full-time Sarah had lots of fun teaching at an Ivy League. Then she realized she could have even more fun writing romance. Her favorite things after writing are adventuring and travel. You'll frequently find her using her degree at a dino dig site, crawling into a cave, snorkeling, or on horseback riding through the jungle – all fodder for her next book. She's lived in Scotland, Norway, Portugal, Switzerland and NYC. She currently lives in the Caribbean with her water-obsessed pup and her awesome family. You can visit her online at www.sarahready.com

Stay up to date, get exclusive epilogues and bonus content. Join Sarah's newsletter at www.sarahready.com/newsletter.